**He shouldn't feel this towards Viv's son. The son whose father was unknown—who surely couldn't be him.**

Surely she would have told him if she'd even suspected it? He couldn't identify what "this" was, but it was too powerful, too...

"What are you doing here?"

His heart stopped as if with a close-range bullet.

Breathless, pulseless, he jerked his head up, around.

And there she was. Viv. In another camouflaging get-up, fresh out of a shower or a bath, hair darkened with wetness, flushed, fragrant even at this distance. And mad as hell that he was here.

It only sent his rioting emotions screeching. How he *hungered* for her. And now he knew how much she'd suffered, how much she'd endured, what she'd triumphed over, how much he'd mistreated her, the hunger was gnawing at him body and soul. And then there was Sam...

**Olivia Gates** has always pursued many passions. But the time came when she had to set up a 'passion priority'—to give her top one her all—and writing won. Hands down.

She is most fulfilled when she is creating worlds and conflicts for her characters and then exploring and untangling them bit by bit, sharing her protagonists' every heartache and hope and heart-pounding doubt until she leads them to their indisputably earned and glorious happy ending.

When she's not writing she is a doctor, a wife to her own alpha male, and a mother to one brilliant girl and one demanding Angora cat. Please visit Olivia at www.oliviagates.com

**Recent titles by the same author:**

DESERT PRINCE, EXPECTANT MOTHER
THE SHEIKH SURGEON'S PROPOSAL

# THE DESERT SURGEON'S SECRET SON

BY
OLIVIA GATES

**MILLS & BOON**
*Pure reading pleasure*™

First published in Great Britain 2008
Large Print edition 2009
Harlequin Mills & Boon Limited,
Eton House, 18-24 Paradise Road,
Richmond, Surrey TW9 1SR

© Olivia Gates 2008

ISBN: 978 0 263 20512 1

Set in Times Roman 16½ on 18½ pt.
17-0509-52775

Printed and bound in Great Britain
by CPI Antony Rowe, Chippenham, Wiltshire

# THE DESERT
# SURGEON'S
# SECRET SON

To my editor, Sheila Hodgson, for doing it yet again—getting the best book out of me.

To my mother, husband and daughter, for the support, enthusiasm and inspiration. Can't do it without you all.

# CHAPTER ONE

SHEIKH GHALEB BEN ABBAS ben Najeeb Aal Omraan fought down another wave of reluctance.

He really needed to get over it. Admit it. That he couldn't be everywhere, do everything himself.

He'd long put being a surgeon and the driving force behind the advancement of Omraania's health system first, but his duties as heir to the throne weren't going anywhere. In fact, his father was pressuring him to be more proactive in matters of state. He'd chosen to press harder during the last months, at a time when his new position as Head of Surgery at Jobail Advanced Medical Center, his crowning project, was threatening to overwhelm his schedule.

He'd resisted the need for someone to share that vital position, the one closest to his heart, from day one. It had taken almost making a fatal mistake during a kind of surgery he'd done in his sleep for years to make him admit he might have been pushing himself too far. Adnan had jumped on the admission, had suggested a replacement head of surgery, amending his suggestion to co-Head at Ghaleb's point-blank refusal. One to have until Ghaleb put matters in order and decided whether to make the position permanent, with the "co" in front of "Head" or without it.

Adnan had put out the ad for the position throughout the medical world, and applications had swamped him. Ghaleb's requirements had easily eliminated most of the applicants and Adnan had flown to the States to interview the few remaining candidates. His choice was arriving today. Right now, actually.

Ghaleb changed direction, heading to Adnan's office instead of to his own private elevator to the surgical floor. He caught him at the door.

Adnan swung around. "I'm going to receive your new co-head of surgery, *Somow'wak,* show her around. Would you like me to schedule a meeting after you finish your list?"

Her? He had nothing against having a female co-head, but it was a matter of statistics that there were more successful male surgeons.

"Don't bother, Adnan," Ghaleb said as he bypassed him, had him almost running to keep up with him as he cleared his personal territory encompassing most of the top floor and swept through the workstations of his immediate staff. "The place to meet my co-head of surgery is in the OR. She doesn't have to impress me with her character, just her surgical skills."

"I'm confident she will, *Somow'wak*. She's the only applicant who answered all your requirements. Her résumé is astounding."

"If she answered *all* my requirements, Adnan, her résumé might be too astounding to be true."

"I truly don't think so, but in the unfortunate situation she doesn't live up to the promise—"

"I'll hold you responsible for wasting my time."

Adnan looked mortified. Ghaleb felt contrite at once. Adnan was his right hand and advisor. His friend. And he had few friends. None really. His position and vocation precluded intimacy, with its demands of time and trust, with its inherent dangers. He'd never been free to choose friends, to risk making errors of judgment. To answer the clamoring of his heart…

Apart from his father, he had only two allies he'd trust with his life. Adnan was one of them. He shouldn't pummel him with his frustration at being forced to admit his limitations.

He gave Adnan's shoulder an apologetic squeeze. "I trust your judgment, Adnan, more than my own sometimes. That's why I let you make this decision for me. But it's no big deal if she doesn't live up to her promise. You'll just renew your search. I can hold out a few more months until you find a replacement."

"*That's* what worries me, *Somow'wak,* not that I wouldn't have lived up to your faith, but that you *can't* hold out under the same strain. You've been juggling responsibilities for too many years that would bring half a dozen men to their knees in months."

"We won't have this debate again, Adnan. I'm taking the most major step in managing these responsibilities, but I'm not going to settle for anything but the best person for the job. Better no help than inferior help."

Adnan knew this was where he fell silent. Ghaleb breathed in relief. He'd ended another confrontation with him. With himself.

He was admitting he'd only postponed it, was about to exit the corridor connecting his inner domain to the floor's reception hall when the momentum of his strides and thoughts faltered, died.

Four of Adnan's aides appeared at the far end of the glass-faceted, soaring-roofed space and walked toward them. They surrounded a statuesque woman in the formation of flanking an honored guest. Everything about the woman bombarded him like punches.

Her clothes impeccable for the climate and culture, their looseness instead of obscuring, showcasing each long limb and ripe curve, each undulation of feminine assurance and fluid grace. The severe bun he just knew would cascade to a waterfall of gleaming buttersscotch when released. The eyes deep-set in self-possession. The features sculpted by a god of beauty. She had the bearing of someone who knew her worth, her effect, exuded it with each breath.

His lungs burned, imploded.

This woman was nothing like the woman who occupied his memory, the creature who'd seemed to have been powered by the sun itself, the intensity and instability of its solar flares emanating from every move of her extra-slim, deeply tanned body, from every flash of her golden eyes, every ripple of the untamed layers of her sun-blazing hair.

But there was no doubt. Not for a second.

That goddess in the distance *was* her.

*Viv.*

The woman who'd shown him what being totally loved felt like, who'd taught him what surrender to emotional and sensual overload meant. The woman he'd thought he'd never be able to live without. The one he'd rushed to that fateful day seven years ago to offer a life by his side here in Omraania, risking so much, only to overhear her saying he'd meant nothing to her.

Viv. The woman he'd been struggling to forget every day of those years. Here. Walking into his center as if she owned it, head held high, looking ahead like a princess in a royal procession, turning every head and turning to no one herself, uncaring of everyone's scrutiny. And unaware of his.

*What was she doing here?*

"Ah, there's Dr. Vivienne LaSalle, right on time."

Adnan's pleased words pummeled him.

*She* was the woman he'd picked to be his co-head of surgery?

Ghaleb staggered back into the shadows, his heart battering his ribs. Adnan turned to him in alarm.

"*Maolai?* Are you all right?"

No, he was *not* all right. He'd never been so shocked in his life. After all these years he'd remained secure she'd forever reside within the boundaries of bitter memory, she was here. In his kingdom, invading his territory, emerging from the shadows of addiction to become reality once more. *Ya Ullah,* how had this happened? She'd applied for the job? Why? She was Adnan's choice? How?

There could be one answer. She'd managed to fool him. Just like she'd managed to fool him when she'd made him pick her for the position of his research assistant. It hadn't been on merit he'd chosen her back then either. He'd taken one look at her, had felt her eating him alive with her eagerness and singeing him with her energy, and he hadn't considered anyone else. He'd been smitten with a glance.

He'd still resisted. How he remembered how he had. He hadn't had time let alone a place in his life for her. But she hadn't taken no for an answer and within days his resolve had disintegrated. He'd touched her and had been consumed body and reason in the conflagration that had followed.

This time he'd relied on Adnan's reason, though she'd clearly tampered with his, as well.

Anger, bitterness and shock roiled with the surge of unquenched hunger. And among the seething, reason struggled to be heard. It cried that the sane course of action was to send her out of Omraania on the spot. Without letting her know he'd seen her.

Without letting her see him.

He was in no condition to listen to reason.

She had a plan, coming here. No doubt the same one she'd had when she'd pursued and seduced him in the past. She'd wanted a life of luxury as his mistress. She'd even begged him for it when he'd come to his senses. Why not give her the chance to play it out? After all, he had to reward such effort, didn't he?

But what he really needed was to see her for what she really was, to erase her generous, guileless image, the persona that existed out of bounds of logic, retaining a viselike hold on him.

What he needed was closure.

He knew how to get it.

He turned on Adnan. "Restart your search for a co-head of surgery. Now."

After a moment of shock at his viciousness, Adnan rushed to say, "*Maolai,* I realize her looks are deceiving. I had the same reaction when I first saw her, thought she couldn't possibly have the experience and stamina to hold such a position, but—"

"But she convinced you otherwise," Ghaleb spat, his vehemence purging a measure of shock and anger, accessing his misplaced equilibrium. "Now she'll have to convince me. Send her to scrub and gown."

Adnan was at a loss now. "So you will still interview her?"

"*I* will start my list," Ghaleb tossed over his shoulder as he strode back to his office. "*You* will restart your search."

Vivienne walked deeper into the medical center touted as the most advanced on the planet, escorted by the four behemoths who made her feel like a head of state who might be assassinated—or a fugitive who might make a run for it—at any second.

She concentrated on regulating her breathing, her steps, stared ahead to ward off the curiosity bombarding her, fought down the waves of nausea and anxiety. And exhaustion.

She'd been in surgery till she'd gone to collect Sam and Anna for the trip here. Then, throughout the thirteen-hour nonstop flight aboard Ghaleb's flying palace, she hadn't had a wink of sleep. She'd set foot in Omraania two hours ago, had barely deposited her family in the lavish accommodation he'd provided before rushing here without pausing.

She'd been stunned by the royal treatment, but Adnan El Khalil, her recruiter, had enlightened her. This wasn't personal. Being Omraania's foremost surgeon and the crown prince's co-head of surgery was a huge deal. Ghaleb would have treated anyone he gave the position to with the same extravagance.

She'd been stunned he'd given it to her, even if she did fit his requirements to a T. She'd applied expecting to be rejected out of hand. When she'd been chosen, she'd been forced to conclude either Ghaleb had forgotten who she was or he didn't consider their past liaison, insignificant to him as it had been, a reason not to accept her when she was the best person for the job.

Now she was in his territory. And though the job description assured her of minimal exposure to him, she was bound to see him.

And she didn't want to see him. Not in this life, not in the next. The man she'd once loved beyond sanity and self-preservation, the man who'd taken everything she'd had to give then walked away, not even sparing her a goodbye.

But anguish at losing him, agony and anger at being so cruelly discarded, had soon ceased to matter. Pregnancy changed a woman's priorities. Having a baby had changed her, period. Forever.

Still hurting from their breakup, she'd forced herself back to her feet. She'd no longer been a woman who'd been trampled on. She was a doctor who'd fought to be the best she could be to provide the best life for her son, and a mother whose life revolved around him.

She'd agonized over whether to tell Ghaleb he'd fathered a son or not. But she couldn't risk it.

As the heir to the throne of a conservative kingdom, Ghaleb had had no place in his life for her beyond the stolen, secret months they'd had together. She hadn't been able to predict what he'd do if he'd learned about Sam. The possibility that he might have taken him away to have him raised to his specifications away from the winds of scandal, had kept her silent. And just like she'd forced herself to realize she hadn't needed him, she'd become convinced Sam wouldn't either. She'd been determined she'd be

all the family Sam needed. And that had been
before she'd been blessed to have her aunt
become a part of their tiny family, too.

But as Sam had grown, so had his questions
about his father. Lately they'd grown more insistent, often bitter, even frantic.

She'd been sorely tempted to tell him his father
was dead, to close that chasm once and for all.
But she couldn't bring herself to say the words,
had spent the last months in an agony of doubt.

Was she being selfish? Was she heeding her
scars and disregarding Sam's needs? If she took
what Ghaleb had done to her out of the equation,
could she believe he'd want to know his child?
And if he did, surely now that Sam was this old
and attached to her, he wouldn't consider taking
him away from her? Maybe they could arrange
something so he'd be in Sam's life? Would Sam's
life be better if Ghaleb was in it? Was it time to
find out the answer to these questions? If it was,
how could she find them out?

Then Ghaleb had started combing the medical
world for a co-head of surgery. Everybody
thought the job an incredible professional and financial opportunity, which it was.

But to her it was a sign, an unrepeatable chance

to enter Omraania for a while, be in Ghaleb's milieu, to make an informed and final decision, one she wouldn't regret. To bring father and son together, or not.

And she was here, and she'd see him again, even if in passing and mainly from afar, and maybe one day soon she'd tell him...

What if his reaction was to treat her with the same contempt he had when she'd offered him *carte blanche* with her life? What if he didn't believe her and all she managed was to sustain another humiliating blow? She couldn't afford injuries now that both Sam and Anna counted on her. What if he did believe her and her worst fears came to pass? What if he snatched Sam and kicked her out?

Had she made a mistake coming here? Was it too late to turn around, take Sam and Anna and run back home?

*Stop it. Breathe. You've been over this a thousand times.*

There was no other way to settle Sam's mind, his future.

She unclenched her fists, inhaled a tremulous breath.

She'd do this. It would be okay. After a no-doubt
brief meeting with the insanely busy Ghaleb,
who wouldn't give her the time of day anyway,
she'd take on the responsibilities of her temporary position where she'd begin gauging his per-
sonality unblinded by the passion that had once
swallowed her whole or by the hatred that had
in the intervening years. She'd observe him from
afar, in his working environment, analyze his
character and predict his actions through his
behavior, through others' view of him. She'd
take her time about coming to a decision how to
proceed…

"Dr. LaSalle. If you'll come this way, please?"

She rose from the depths of chaos to find Adnan
two feet away from her. She'd been looking
through him for what seemed like a while now.

She blinked, croaked, "What?"

"I'm sorry if I've spoken too fast, Dr.
LaSalle," the lanky, dark man said in an impeccable British accent much like Ghaleb's, though
his was devoid of the exotic inflections and
intense undertones that had turned Ghaleb's into
a hypnotic weapon. "I was anxious to inform
you of the surgery list awaiting you."

"Surgery list?" she rasped, her voice roughened by disuse and confusion. "But we were supposed to have a reconnaissance tour—"

"We will have one later," Adnan cut in smoothly. "Right now there's been a change of plan."

*But there couldn't be,* she almost cried out.

She had counted on everything going according to plan. If that was changing already, she didn't know what she'd do, and it had to be Ghaleb who'd changed them… *God, why?*

*Calm down.* "Is there an emergency?" she asked.

"No, Dr. LaSalle." Adnan gestured for her to precede him.

So it wasn't a situation where he needed every surgeon around to pitch in. So maybe he wanted her to get to work at once?

No matter what his reasons were, she had no choice but to comply.

Her love for Sam made sure of that. It would make her do anything. Even letting Ghaleb pull her strings again.

She gritted her teeth and let herself be pulled.


Ghaleb looked down at his hands, gripping the edges of the stainless-steel sink, fascinated by how white his knuckles were. F/0233419

Any minute now his plan would unfold.

If he could call the impulse he'd acted on a plan.

Not that ten more days of contemplation would have afforded him a better course of action.

After all, Viv was here to be co-Head Surgeon no less, wasn't she? Then she had to abide by the test he'd had in store for said co-Head. Let them meet across the operating table so she'd show him her qualifications, or lack of them, at once.

He had no doubt it would be a lack he'd uncover.

During their time together they hadn't worked together much, and never in the OR. He'd heard of her proficiency as a surgeon but hadn't seen evidence of it himself. He'd concluded it had been her father's influence as financial director of the hospital where she'd worked that had gotten her good reports and opportunities. She'd boosted the latter with her beauty and charisma. Hadn't she made him give her a position he could have given to a dozen others who would have done it more justice? A position it had become clear she'd fought for to be near him, to seduce him? And once she had, work had been the last thing on his mind, too.

Now she'd conned her way into another position. One he didn't believe for a second she fit, as she'd proclaimed she did. Still, with him there to make sure she did no damage, he was interested to see her try to live up to her claims.

And fail miserably.

That way, it wouldn't be personal history or preconceptions that decided him against hiring her. He wanted it to be her inadequacy. He'd see for himself how much of that résumé of hers was fabricated. Then he'd close her chapter forever....

All his hair stood on end, as if he'd been doused in a field of static electricity. A presence. Unmistakable even after all these years. Viv.

Every caution told him not to move, to let her initiate the confrontation. Every instinct screamed for him to turn, catch that moment when she was as off guard as he was. It was the hot, sharp sound that spilled from lips he knew to be rose-soft and cherry-tinted, which had once wrung incoherence from him in soul-wrenching kisses and moans, that shattered the stalemate.

He swung around. And déjà vu engulfed him whole.

Time rewound to that moment he'd first laid eyes on her. When she'd gotten him alone in another scrubbing/gowning anteroom, in another life, to convince him to choose her.

Had he brought her here to reenact their first meeting? Had she somehow made him do it?

Anything seemed possible as some override function inside him ignored mental commands, urging his senses to roam her, feast on her, relive again the unrepeatable attraction. It was as if everything that had happened since the last time he'd left her arms had been erased. It was as if it would be the most natural thing in the world to surge toward her, that she'd rush to a halfway melding, all the sooner to get lost in each other's arms.

She stood as transfixed as him, her eyes wide in shock as great as his. And, he could swear, as genuine.

The conviction jogged him out of the surreal timelessness where nothing had gone wrong between them to the distasteful present with its preposterousness.

Shocked? When she was here in full premeditation?

But no. She *was* shocked. This was no act. Not any more than his own loss of control, his own plunge into that time warp.

So what did it all mean?

He exhaled the breath trapped in his lungs, admitted he had no grasp of this situation, much less control over it. He turned fully to her, stood straighter, preparing for the inevitable. The passing of shock and what must follow of her old methods of enticement and seduction.

But what was this, surging inside him, shocking him again with its power? Eagerness?. Did he actually want to see blatant invitation in her eyes, in her stance, in the way she'd call his name as if to say, *Take me, ravish me, finish me, now?*

He licked parched lips, counting down the seconds before her gaze heated, her posture relaxed, beckoned...

"So, we meet again, Dr. Aal Omraan. Or do you only answer to His Royal Highness Crown Prince Ghaleb now?"

# CHAPTER TWO

GHALEB COULD ONLY STARE at the woman who no longer resembled Viv beyond the basics.

She pursed her lips as the last of the shock he'd detected drained, steel replacing it. "I assume it was you who ordered me to report to the OR?"

*B'hag'gejaheem*—by hell, what was going on here?

Her voice was the same, velvety and rich like chocolate and red wine, but he'd never imagined it could sound so… cold. And that was nothing to how those whiskey eyes swept him as if examining an uncertain specimen and finding it deplorably wanting.

"Of course it was you." She answered her own question with a flick of an elegant hand. "I've been here only two hours and I already realize nobody breathes here without your say-so, let alone thinks, speaks or acts." She let go of his gaze, as if she found nothing about him of interest, hers sweeping around for something worthy of her attention. "I assume you want me to scrub?"

The answer that almost escaped his lips was, *I want you to tell me who you are, and where Viv, the old Viv, is.*

Where was the woman who'd fluttered around him, inundating him with hunger and appreciation? Though it had been an act, why wasn't she continuing it now?

From experience he knew women went to any lengths to capture or resurrect prosperous men's interests. And as one of the richest men in the world, a royal and a celebrated surgeon to boot, he defined prosperity, was one of the most vigorously pursued.

So was this her new act? The one she'd determined would reignite his interest?

If it was, it was succeeding. Spectacularly.

And why not? He'd play it her way. He'd give her all the rope she needed to hang herself. Then, when he'd had the satisfaction of looking her in the eye and reading her admission of defeat, he'd send her out of Omraania, out of his life. This time forever.

"Your assumptions are correct," he finally drawled, advancing on her in steps he hoped looked measured when they were, in fact, impeded by lingering upheaval. "Those concerning yourself. I assure you I don't surround myself with automatons or thralls."

"Sure. Thanks for sharing that." Sarcasm? He couldn't be sure with her face and voice expressionless. "Will you, please, send your head non-automaton non-thrall to direct me to the OR where I'm needed after I've scrubbed? I'll be exactly ten minutes."

Sarcasm. His lips twitched, not on mirth, on indecision how to react. "Adnan isn't one of my medical personnel. His role ended when he escorted you here. I'll take over from here."

"Fine. Whatever." She moved toward one of the lockers. "So, what's on the list this morning?"

"Ten surgeries."

She didn't bat a lid as she removed her jacket, exposing a sleeveless beige blouse. He came to a stop, his gaze trapped by the perfection of her arms. And even in these sterile surroundings, with everything else making erotic thoughts out of bounds, lust kicked in his loins. His mouth watered.

Seemingly oblivious to his state, she strode to the nearest sink, picked up a prepackaged, presterilized brush impregnated with surgical detergent, held her hands below the tap for the infrared sensor to kick in. "Care to elaborate?"

He tamped down the urge to stride to her, take her by those arms, run stinging-for-their-softness hands all over them before branding them with his tongue and teeth, tasting their cream, biting into their vitality.

*Ya Ullah,* he shouldn't have abstained from feminine pleasures for so long. Now he was starved.

But no. He hadn't been. Not until he'd seen her. So mental aversion hadn't even dulled the sharpness of the hunger. So he hadn't been cured, had only been an addict forced to abstain...

"Six minimally invasive procedures." He supplied the answer a raised eyebrow pressed for, struggling to imbue his voice with a tone as offhand as hers. "Vascular and thoracic, one lumpectomy and one simple mastectomy, and two second-stage damage-control surgeries. All up your street, I believe?"

She nodded without looking at him as she wet her forearms to the elbows, assurance itself. "Dead center, yes."

Then she began to scrub. Just as he felt he'd disappeared from her senses' radar, she raised her eyes. "You have someone around to help me gown, or shall I go the solo route?"

He couldn't answer right away. Not when his mind was being swamped with all the times he'd ungowned her, so to speak, exposing her to his impatience and hunger.

When he answered, his voice sounded like raking through gravel. "I'll gown you."

That exquisite eyebrow rose again. Had she heard the gruffness, known its import?

But her gaze wasn't taunting, or knowing. It was empty. "I know I'm here to share a position with you, but isn't gowning me taking the coworker thing outside the job description?"

*Share a position.* A thousand images inundated him, of every position he'd shared with her, the ecstasy they'd wrung from each other's bodies in each. Had she meant the double entendre?

No. She hadn't. He was sure her comment had been professional. If her dismissal of his authority could be called that. But there was no sexual innuendo in anything she said or did. *Or* she was a more undetectable actress than he'd imagined.

Thinking a closer look might avail him of better judgment, he closed in on her. "I assure you that helping fellow surgeons gown isn't outside my job parameters."

She finished scrubbing, held up her hands to drip-dry before picking up a sterile towel folded over the gown/glove packs and began a flawless drying technique. "Really? So does Crown Prince and Head of Surgery have Scrub Nurse or Circulator in the fine print of expected duties? Who would have thought?"

A jolt coursed through him again. No one talked to him like that. Ever. Not even her. Especially her. Not in the past.

But why the jolts? Had he come to expect deference beyond decorum and professionalism that it shocked him she was speaking freely in his presence? Admittedly, he hadn't been approachable in recent years, but had she been right? Had he gone beyond maintaining the distance his status demanded into imposing a form of oppression?

Not that she was affected by whatever intimidation he emitted. She hurled out her thoughts as they formed.

"Isn't life full of surprises?" he drawled, almost to himself.

She volunteered no answer to that but reached

for a gown and began unfolding it, her sterile procedure perfect.

He advanced on her then, unable to stay away a second longer. The closer he got, the worse it got. Her scent reached out to him, enveloped him. Yes. This was *it*. Unchanged. Sweet and fragrant and exuding sensuality.

He reached her as she placed her arms inside the sleeves, circled her in one aching sweep, careful not to come into contact with any part of her. For sterile conditions, he told himself.

He began adjusting her scrubs around her lush body, focused on regulating his breathing, his urges. She stood there all through, eyes downcast, seemingly unbreathing.

He was tightening her belt when his surgical team entered the hall en masse.

He almost groaned in disappointment. Now he'd have no excuse to demand that she return the favor. She was already moving away, snapping on gloves on her own.

Resigned that this interlude had come to an end, that this face-off had gone against his expectations and certainly in her favor, he turned to his own scrubbing and gowning, acutely conscious of her every movement, every breath.

In minutes he turned to her again, impatient to continue his study of her—and sustained another shock.

She was smiling. At anesthesiologist Hisham Sukhr and resident Aneesah Othman. She hadn't smiled at *him* since she'd walked into the hall. Not even a mockery of a formality.

She'd *never* smiled at him like that.

And he suddenly realized what had been missing from the smiles she'd once lavished on him. This, what flowed from her smile right now. Ease. She'd always been…tense, even forced, for the lack of more appropriate words, around him.

Had it been a manifestation of the artifice she'd practiced? Looking at her now, it was impossible to believe she was *capable* of artifice. Which was too stupid a thing to think.

Even more stupid was the surge of anger and animosity he felt as he watched the scene unfold. Anger toward her for showing him how delightful her ease was, but that he'd never warranted it. Animosity toward Hisham, his most trusted anesthesiologist, whose eyes sparkled with the covetous thoughts any male would have about Viv…

*Ya Ullah.* Was he on the verge of a breakdown,

as Adnan insisted he was? Was he angry at Viv for not being cordial with him? Was he jealous that another man coveted her on sight? When in either case he should expect nothing less, nothing else?

It was time to put an end to this stupidity, get on with his plans. Before he forgot what they were and why he'd hatched them.

He moved to the door connecting to the OR he'd chosen. As the door slid open, he turned and a hush fell over the buzzing room.

"Now that Dr. LaSalle has introduced herself, we're ready to start our list." With that, he entered the OR.

Everyone followed in a silence loud with surprise that he hadn't given Viv the esteem of a formal introduction and welcome in front of her future team and subordinates. From her there was only opacity. She'd closed her mind to him.

Viv walked into the OR last, struggling not to wobble.

This wasn't what was supposed to happen.

She'd accepted the position because it dictated she'd meet Ghaleb possibly a couple of times initially, to set things up, then she wouldn't see him again as she did his job when he wasn't around. He shouldn't be here, about to begin a ten-surgery list with her. Why wasn't he leaving her to it?

This *had* to be a test. One he would have subjected anyone he'd install as his co-head to. A one-off. Yes. She could live with that. She thought. She hoped. If she survived the next hours…

*Stop it.* Why was she going to pieces like this?

But she knew why, didn't she? She'd entered to scrub, had seen him standing there with his back to her, and it had been like being catapulted back to the past, to that time she'd sought him out, to sell him on choosing her for his research assistant's position.

She'd seen him many times from afar till that moment, each time suffering a jolt of awareness at the power and charisma compounding the impact of his phenomenal looks and physique. She'd known he had the same effect on every female with a heartbeat, but had been convinced one close-up look would take care of all that.

Then he'd turned to her and her self-assurance had boiled and evaporated, then his answering awareness had turned hers into compulsion. She'd hurled herself at him, a moth fully aware of its fiery end yet hurtling deliriously toward the flame. Then he'd left her and her world had turned upside down. It had taken months to set it right. How could she let herself be taken by storm again?

Oh, she knew how. This time he'd turned to her only to show her her memories had been merciful. Or the years had been cruel, conspiring with maturity to chisel his physique to godlike perfection, hone his beauty and effect to lacerating levels.

She didn't know how she'd looked at him, answered back. She guessed she'd launched into sarcastic mode, her automatic defense mechanism when overwhelmed. She barely remembered what she'd said, all her focus on keeping her face and tone empty so she hadn't betrayed her upheaval to his scrutiny.

And, damn him, he'd scrutinized. His eyes, the eyes she would once have done anything to see igniting with approval, with passion, had left her face, only to travel over her, leaving burn marks wherever they landed, scorching away her hard-won stability.

While he'd been as stable as a mountain, betraying nothing at the sight of her but the certainty that he remembered her, and the same indifference with which he'd ignored her offer of her life to mess up for as long as he pleased. Then, as if he hadn't treated her like a leper, as if they'd never even met before, her pitiful barbs breaking off his force field of assurance and superiority, he'd approached her like an inexorable storm, rattling every cell in her body with alarm and awareness. Then he'd *gowned* her.

He'd circled her, like a predator biding his time, giving his prey a nervous breakdown wondering if he'd pounce at once or if he was sated and was only playing, would prolong the sadistic game until he was hungry again. He'd let her feel him, quake with his nearness, had flayed her with his breath, his scent, his hands hovering over a body that was suddenly a battleground for every forbidden hunger and recollection, tugging at her with strings made of her gown's ties, her cruel memory and his far more pitiless reality.

She didn't know how she'd remained on her feet.

She had to stay away from him. For the time she was here, and until she reached a decision. She couldn't let his effect tamper with her logic and self-control again. Sam. She was here for Sam.

But she couldn't stay away right now. He was looking at her, clearly summoning her.

Rigid, grudging steps brought her opposite him, across the table he'd elected, as the well-oiled machine of his surgical team brought in the first two patients, placing one in front of them.

She cast her gaze to the patient being placed at the next station. She may be here to settle a personal issue, but she'd also signed a contract, had made a commitment to do the best job she could, as she always did. She'd better locate her misplaced composure and professionalism.

She gulped down a steadying breath, forced her eyes to seek his. The moment those obsidian infernos slammed into her she was tempted to say *Let the test begin* or *Do your worst*.

Instead, she said, "Where do you want me?"

*Back in my office, spread on my desk, naked and open and begging for me.*

Ghaleb gritted his teeth. These lust attacks were getting preposterous. And infuriating.

He harnessed his anger—at her for the weakness only she had ever engendered in him, at himself for letting her still wield that power—and emptied his gaze. "I want you right here."

"You mean I'll take this patient?"

"I mean you'll work with me on this patient."

"Two patients, two so-called head surgeons handling one. Anything wrong with that picture, I wonder?"

"We'll handle every patient together. Es-Sayed Elwan in station two was brought in now because it'll take the length of es-Sayedah Afaf's operation to get him prepped."

She gave him a glance that made him feel she was probing him, fathoming his motivations.

Then, without giving away her conclusions, she turned to their sedated patient, took in the field of surgery being prepped. "So, what will it be for her? Lumpectomy or simple mastectomy?"

"Lumpectomy." He asked for their patient's films to be clipped on the backlit screen feet away. Viv examined them.

She was back in a minute. "Localized tumor in a breast with no signs of lymph-node involvement." She murmured her diagnosis, mirroring his. "Perfect for a breast-conserving procedure. Will she have radiation of the rest of the breast afterwards, or is the lumpectomy the limit of her treatment?"

"Why do you ask?"

She shrugged as she examined the woman's breast, translating X-ray evidence into the physical one. "I ask because she must be over seventy and some schools of treatment think radiation doesn't offer a better prognosis for her age group. I don't know if your center subscribes to this belief or not."

"What would be your recommendation?"

"Radiation afterwards, no question, if her general condition allows it. Even though women of her age are said not to be at risk of a hormonally induced recurrence and therefore wouldn't benefit from radiation while risking a higher incidence of its side effects, recent research overwhelmingly proves those receiving radiation remain free of cancer longer than women who don't."

"And what do you think my center opts for?"

"How would I know? You may be the most advanced center in the world but I've seen many who run a close second who suffer from unchanging attitudes and biases toward new research. Superiority spawns prejudice, not to mention an all-knowing streak and the tendency to play God."

And that *had* to be a double entendre. Making reference to the way he'd walked away from her?

He didn't see a connection but was certain this summation wasn't all about the pompous and misguided decisions and views many highly regarded surgeons and medical establishments made and advertised.

Unable to fathom the rebuff he felt singeing him, he drawled, "Let me assure you that at the Jobail Advanced Medical Center we embrace all substantiated research and commit a major part of our resources, human and financial, to furthering said research and to cementing its results into facts. Radiation after lumpectomy for older women is our recommendation."

She only gave a nod, continued examining the patient.

Just like that? No comment? No more digs?

No. None. Was that what she'd become? Not given to saying a word more than necessary? Closing a subject once it had been satisfactorily resolved? What had happened to cause that reversal? Where had the gushing, hyperactive, excitable young woman gone? Where had this serene, stable and centered woman sprung from?

And was now the time to ponder such mysteries, *ya ghabbi?*

Exhaling his frustration, he murmured for a scalpel. Once it was in his palm, he stared at it.

He'd almost forgotten his plan. Now he remembered, he no longer wanted to go through with it.

Before he gave in to another impulse, he extended the scalpel to her. "You do the honors."

She didn't spare him a glance as she palmed the scalpel, adjusted her position. Before he opened his mouth, she made a sure-handed incision around the areola. The approach he hadn't had time to recommend, maximizing accessibility to the tumor.

He moved forward, tension draining by degrees as he fell into step with her, assisting her as she accessed the tumor and extracted it with a surrounding layer of healthy tissue, somehow managing to leave the breast looking untouched.

She placed the specimen in a collection vial and one of his nurses hurried with it to the adjacent lab. Viv turned her eyes to him, all he could see of her behind her mask.

"We'll have our verdict in minutes," he murmured. "You can move on to the next step while we wait."

She at once made an incision in their patient's armpit.

He tensed. "Removing the axillary lymph nodes?"

"I'm going for sentinel node biopsy." She paused. "You have a different course of action?"

He didn't. He gestured for her to go ahead.

She started dissecting the first node. His muscles tightened, ready to jump in. This was where surgeons of less than extensive experience messed up. But with every fluid, precise movement of her hands his tension eased. He couldn't have done it better.

After he sent another nurse to the lab with the nodes, they spent the following minutes exchanging opinions.

The nurses came back with a favorable verdict and the rest of his tension dissipated. It ratcheted up again at Viv's tremulous exhalation. He studied her, gauged her reaction.

Yes. There it was. Unmistakable. What echoed inside him.

She validated his analysis when she murmured, "Now I can hope this procedure will be the last es-Sayedah Afaf will suffer on account of that tumor."

He muttered his corroboration. And as if to show him that was of no consequence to her, she removed the drain he'd inserted, murmured for suturing materials, then proceeded to give es-Sayedah Afaf one of the most undetectable suture jobs he'd ever seen.

They finally pulled back from the table, leaving the others to wrap up, and Viv slipped from the chair she'd asked for in mid-surgery and stretched her back. His eyes clung to her movements, each accessing memories of nights when he'd massaged that resilient back, luxuriating in her feel, in her pleasure, before he'd mounted her, given her what by then she'd been whimpering for….

He remained seated. He'd remain seated until she'd long left the OR, otherwise he'd have a scandal on his hands.

He realized she was looking at him when his face began to burn. He swung his eyes back to her, found her gaze on him, steady, neutral. Then she only said, "Next."

And for the next ten hours, even forgoing a lunch break, they went through the varied, demanding list. By the time their last patient was wheeled to Resuscitation, there was no doubt in his mind anymore.

Doubts had started to crumble with that first incision she'd made. From then on, as she'd passed every test he'd thrown at her with ease and confidence, they'd disintegrated faster. They now lay pulverized at his feet. He had the verdict of his own eyes.

The only thing she'd been guilty of had probably been to understate her skills. As a diagnostician she was uncanny; as a surgeon she was unparalleled.

And he couldn't believe how much that upset him.

It meant she really could just be here for the job.

Everything validated this theory. Her every nuance said she'd become the opposite of her old accommodating, approval-seeking self. Her antagonism had been superbly leashed in front of those she believed she'd oversee, but it had been unmistakable to him. And it was no act to whet his interest. His approval *was* the last thing she coveted. And it outraged him.

It was contrary of him when he had every reason not to wish for any personal reaction or interaction with her.

But now she was withholding it he wanted it, had to have it.

He *would* have it.

He would also find out how she'd become the woman who'd stood up to him, who'd surprised him at every turn, the woman he'd depended on through some of the most demanding surgeries possible.

And when he did so, he'd find out what her game was this time. He was certain there was far more than met the eye to Dr. Vivienne LaSalle.

But her secrets *would* be surrendered. He wouldn't think of a next step until he was in possession of every last one.

Viv staggered into the—thankfully deserted—ladies' room, groped for the support of the nearest solid surface.

Her hand slipped off the quartz vanity top. She barely steadied herself then met her reflection in the mirror—and gasped.

It was like looking at the worst days of her life.

She looked nothing like the scrawny, sunburned, crackling-with-need woman Ghaleb had used and discarded. It was her expression—the vulnerability, the despondency she'd become resigned to after Ghaleb had left and throughout her pregnancy.

Bile rose, mortification splashing through her system, melting the grip of resurrected insecurity and misery.

She was damned if she'd let herself sink back

into those. She was double-damned if she let him affect her this way, or at all.

But, damn it all, he did affect her. Worse than before. He got to her so badly she'd had to ask for a chair during surgery for the first time ever, murmuring something stupid about jet lag.

It seemed absolute power and endless privileges agreed more and more with Ghaleb the longer he had them. And he knew his effect, used it.

One thing made it all bearable. She'd passed his test. And then some. She'd almost had a nervous breakdown holding up under his pressure, but she had. She let reaction rack her now.

In hindsight, she would have preferred it if he'd forgotten her name, had hired her unaware it was her then been enraged at seeing her and sent her out of Omraania on the spot. The more she thought of it, the more she didn't understand why he *had* hired her for such a position when he'd once thought her beneath the position she'd begged him for, that of a mistress he would frequent on his infrequent visits to the U.S. Was he really that detached and professional?

What was going on in that convoluted mind of his?

One thing she knew. If she'd thought meeting

him again would settle her mind, she'd been catastrophically wrong.

She lowered her head to the sink and the tap turned on. Water streamed over her face, warm yet still cooling her burning skin…

"Are you okay, Doctorah Vivienne?"

She inhaled water, jackknifed up spluttering, found a pile of paper towels being shoved into her hands. She dried her watering eyes, focused on the younger woman with exquisite dark eyes and exotic features. The surgical resident whose name she'd forgotten.

God, that was all she needed. To cultivate a reputation for being a spaced-out lightweight among the people she was supposed to spend her two months in purgatory leading.

"I'm so sorry I startled you." The woman looked contrite. "I heard you moaning and got worried."

Viv forced a bright smile. "It's jet lag catching up with me."

The woman smiled back at her. "I can't imagine how you lasted ten hours without a break, and with jet lag, too. I thought no one but Somow'wel Ameer Ghaleb was capable of such staying power."

At hearing Ghaleb's name, her stomach gave a violent lurch.

She pressed a hand to it, forced another smile. "That must be hunger rearing its head, too. I'd better go and catch a bite to eat."

"There are some of the best restaurants in Omraania here in the center. And before you go, let me tell you how great it was to see you at work. I'm now really excited about your appointment."

Pleasure bubbled at her sincerity. Maybe today hadn't been a total disaster after all. First successful surgeries, now an ally.

For the first time since she'd set foot in Omraania her smile turned genuine. "Thanks...uh...Dr. Ani—Anai—"

"Aneesah," she supplied. "It means soothing companion."

Viv's smile widened. "I bet you are, too. Literally your name. You just made my day a hell of a lot better. Thanks again."

Aneesah chuckled and headed farther into the ladies' room. "Anytime, Doctorah Vivienne. See you in surgery."

Viv watched her, her tension draining. She *was* soothing. Nothing seemed as bad as it had minutes ago. She was probably overreacting with exhaustion anyway. It was also normal to feel drained after a confrontation she'd been dreading for years. Sleep would cure everything. Tomorrow she'd figure out her next step.

She put on her jacket as she walked to the foyer, this time noticing every detail, marveling at the intricate patterns on the marble floor, the designs paneling the walls, the gigantic flower arrangement on the centerpiece *fer forgé* table. What did hotels look like here if a medical center was this luxurious? The medical facilities were a century ahead of anything she'd ever worked in, too. As for their accommodations, Sam and Anna had flipped when they'd seen where they'd spend the next two months.

Maybe she should adopt their attitude. Maybe it was the key to surviving this experience. Considering it an interlude, going with the flow, hoping for the best… Yeah, right.

Still following the patterns on the floor, she cleared the automatic doors, only for her gaze to stumble on large feet in camel-colored shoes, planted wide apart.

Without volition, her gaze traveled up the endless legs and powerful thighs attached to them, encased in superbly cut same-colored pants, hands deep in their pockets, stretching the fabric over the potency that had once…

She dragged her eyes up farther, only for them to cling to a black shirt covering an abdomen and chest forged from steel, three buttons left open to expose the mat of silky hair she'd once lost herself to the luxury of threading her fingers through, that had once settled on her breasts, chafing her into a frenzy...

She tore her gaze up to his, found him watching her.

As soon as he gauged he had her attention where he wanted it, he drawled, "I've designated a driver for you. He'll be at your disposal 24/7. He'll now escort you to your new residence. Since it's a quarter to seven now, you should be there by a quarter past. I trust you can get ready in an hour?"

She replayed his question in her mind. It still made no sense. She swallowed, croaked, "Ready? For what?"

"For our working dinner. At eight-fifteen sharp." Before she could say anything, he turned away. Just before he'd gone out of hearing range, he threw over his back, "Be ready."

# CHAPTER THREE

BE READY.

The order reverberated in Viv's mind until she was ready to scream. He'd tossed it at her, expected her to abide by it.

But what did she expect from a despot anyway? Sure, he enveloped it all in layers of benevolence, modernism and tolerance, but in reality he was the same as his desert-raider ancestors, tyrannical rulers and decadent sultans all. Aarrghhh...

*Okay. Enough of that.* She should concentrate on something else. The magnificence of Jobail at sunset, for instance. She may as well enjoy it. Driving through the city that had materialized out of architects' fantasies, cocooned in that rarefied atmosphere of a limo of a level of luxury she hadn't known existed. Without the evidence of her eyes, the sight of the city rushing by, she could have sworn they weren't moving at all. So smooth were the roads...

It wasn't working. And it was Ghaleb's fault.

It was his fault she was victim to volcanic emotions once more after she'd long mastered herself, found tranquility, enjoyed the rewards of control. And all he'd had to do to achieve this reversion had been to expose her to the sight of him, his voice and scent, to breathe near her, look at her. To utter those two words.

She closed her eyes. She should consider this not succumbing to his order but strategic acceptance of an opportunity. This dinner could provide her with time in his company to decide how to proceed. Yes. She could live with that.

Nodding to herself, settling back into the frame of mind she'd accomplished in the past seven years, she opened her eyes as the villa Ghaleb had provided for her came into view at the end of the palm-tree-lined street. A three-story building that could house thirty people, not only three, nestling among at least five acres of impeccably landscaped grounds. It looked far more beautiful now as spotlights showcased each detail in an ingenious play of light and shadows.

Guards opened the remote-controlled gates and the limo slid in through, traveling at least two hundred meters before coming to a stop in front of the villa's main door.

Before she could move, her driver opened her door. She hadn't known anyone, especially someone of his size, could move that fast!

He stood aside, awaiting her exit from the vehicle. He hadn't said one word to her so far. In fact, she hadn't even really been aware of the guy. That was saying something with him so imposing.

That cloak of invisibility must be Ghaleb's conditioning. That really clashed with his assertion that his people possessed independent wills.

Well, she wouldn't treat her driver as if he were some advanced piece of hardware to operate her car and run her errands.

She stepped down from the car and didn't walk away, but turned to face him. He did a double take then resumed looking ahead, but she could see him tensing.

What did he think? That she'd blast him over some imaginary mistake? Was that how Ghaleb kept his subordinates functioning to optimum capacity? Browbeating them with unreasonableness, never satisfied with any level of competence they achieved?

Not that she'd noticed any bullying today. Ghaleb had just murmured a word and his team had met his demands with a speed and efficiency any genie would have envied. And if something inside her whispered that Ghaleb had never needed intimidation of any sort to get what he wanted, that without even trying he'd had her falling over herself to please him, she smothered it. Viciously.

She looked way up at him and smiled. "I just wanted to thank you for the smoothest ride of my life."

The man blinked, seemingly stunned that she'd addressed him at all, and with thanks no less.

He finally rumbled gruffly, "It's my job, *ya sayedati.*"

"It's only right to be thanked for a job well done, uh..." She flashed him an apologetic smile. "I don't know your name yet."

He hesitated again. "Khadamek Abdur-Ruhman."

She didn't get the first word, but knew the second was a name, one of those starting with "Abd," slave or worshipper—of Ullah, of course, in this case one of His other ninety-nine names.

Unsure if the first word was his first name, she made note to ask about it later and extended her hand. "And I'm Vivienne LaSalle."

He barely touched it before withdrawing his own, dark color staining his intimidating face. And she realized.

This guy wasn't only under orders to treat her like some sanctified entity. His culture was vastly different than hers and he—who by the silver band on his left ring finger was married—really was unsure how to deal with women who weren't part of his family. All that coarse maleness was just a misleading exterior. He was out of his depth here, was actually blushing!

She smiled at him again. "I will call you in good enough time when I need you to drive me to work."

"But…*ya sayedati,* you won't need to. I'll be right here in the service houses in the grounds of the villa with the guards."

"Why?" she exclaimed. "Even if you live on the other side of Jobail, you'd get here in less than an hour. In days I'll have a schedule and won't even need to call you!"

"You'll need me for more than commuting to and from work, and you have family with you. They'll need me when you're at work."

"They can also use a phone to call you if they can't use the incredibly efficient public transportation. No. You spend your nights with your family. I will call you, well ahead of time, when I need you. And that's final." He gave her a pained look. He was about to say he couldn't do as she asked. She knew why. Ghaleb. Well, tough. If Ghaleb thought having an enslaved driver would impress her, he was in for a surprise. "It's *final*," she ground out. "I'll tell Prince Ghaleb. Now, go home. Please."

She waved goodbye and turned away, but could tell he remained there until she'd reached the second floor. She was passing along the corridor leading to the bedroom Sam had chosen when she heard the purr of the limo. She wondered if he'd do as she'd demanded or if his orders would prevent him from obeying anyone but Ghaleb. Yet another bone to pick with said prince.

She opened the door to Sam's room, tiptoed in. Not that she needed to. The thickest carpets she'd ever walked on made her steps soundless. But she couldn't be too careful. Sam was a very light sleeper. Like his father. She'd once asked Ghaleb if he ever slept properly, or if he only closed his eyes and pretended to. She'd only had to breathe more deeply as she'd watched him sleep for his eyes to snap open, alert, focused, devouring...

She'd long added this inherited trait to her resentment against Ghaleb. It made her unable to kiss Sam while he slept.

But tonight she couldn't help it. She had to touch him, smell him. Feel his precious life. She needed the strength that connecting with him always gave her. The strength to take on the world and win. She was going to take on something far more cruel tonight. Ghaleb. And her own resurrected weaknesses.

She came down on the mattress Sam had given a test the best trampoline wouldn't have passed, and he didn't stir. A tingle of anxiety slithered down her nerves. She bent closer, inhaled his sweet, beloved scent then touched her lips to his downy cheek. He gave no reaction and panic slammed into her.

She groped for his pulse with one shaking hand and for the bedside light with the other.

"Mo-*om*... Sleepy... Don't wanna go to school..."

Viv sobbed, hiccupped, her eyes watering. And she couldn't hold back. She swept him into her arms in a fierce hug, to grumpier protestations. She let out a chuckle of distress.

"No school, darling. Mom just missed kissing you goodnight."

He cracked one eye open. "You've kissed me ten times now."

And she laughed. "You were counting?"

He buried his head under the pillow, mumbled what sounded like, "Wasn't...too many...too fast...give you more...when I wake up..."

She chuckled, turned off the lamp, took the pillow off his head, put it back under him, kissed him and hurried from the room.

Once outside, she leaned on the door. She was in worse shape than she'd realized. She was obsessive where Sam's safety was concerned but that attack of suffocating dread was a new level.

She looked at her watch. She had exactly thirty-five minutes until Ghaleb's eight-fifteen deadline!

She started to run before she caught herself then stopped, stared into space. What was she *doing,* rushing to make his appointment? She'd take a bath, wash her hair, dry it, dress at leisure. Whomever he sent to fetch her would just have to wait.

Even with this resolution, she had to force

herself not to hurry to her room. And she'd thought her driver—Abdur-Ruhman until proven otherwise—programmed? When she couldn't rise above her own programming? To give Ghaleb anything he wanted?

*No.* Just to be punctual, to strive to fulfill others' expectations. Even when she didn't have a hand in creating those.

She entered the large, cheery room she'd picked haphazardly that morning, again getting only impressions of soft pastel colors and floral designs, having no time to take stock of her surroundings. She collected her things, headed into the plush bathroom and started filling the huge tub, muttering to herself all through the rushed procedure.

And, no, it *wasn't* rushed on account of wanting to fulfill Ghaleb's expectations. She'd become a time freak, as her colleagues called her, so she'd squeeze all the time-consuming things she had to do into each twenty-four hours. She'd bet she couldn't soak or take time to style her hair if she tried.

In thirty minutes she was bathed, dried, body and hair, and dressed. Damn. She wouldn't make Ghaleb wait. But…she *could* lie down in bed until she was fashionably late.

She shook her head at that idea. The moment she hit the bed she'd plunge into a coma. She didn't want to be *that* late.

A melodious bell rang. She sighed, squared her shoulders. On the strike of the minute. Still painfully punctual, huh? A condition he'd clearly imposed on the lackeys sent to fetch her.

She forced herself not to run down the stairs.

The bell rang again. What did those guys expect? That she'd be propped behind the door, waiting for their arrival? Sheesh.

She reached the door, struggled to wipe the frown from her face as she opened it. She couldn't be annoyed with Ghaleb's underlings for being anxious to fulfill their master's orders.

Next moment her heart emptied of blood, her mind of thoughts.

Not underlings on her doorstep... Him...here...

*Ghaleb.* Obsidian eyes drilling into her, taking her apart a cell at a time, ruthlessly sensuous mouth set, sculpted bone structure showcased by the lights illuminating her entrance, body molded in the darkness of the first formal suit she'd seen him in, handmade, detail-worshipping pure silk, looking so good it was unfair...

*As unfair as him popping up on her doorstep like that.*

Anger chased away paralysis. Hoping she hadn't gawked at him for too long and thanking God that Sam and Anna were asleep, she raised her chin and glared at him.

"What happened to your army of errand boys?"

Ghaleb stared at Viv, once again unable to breathe.

The scent of cleanliness and femininity had sizzled into his lungs the moment she'd opened the door. He didn't dare draw another breath laden with her uniqueness before he'd dealt with the first dose. Before he dealt with the response that laying eyes on her again had ripped from his depths.

And he'd been hoping his earlier response had been exaggerated by shock? If anything, it had been dampened by it.

He crackled with her nearness, with the on-slaught of her every detail. The ripeness encased in another neutral-colored creation that made his hands sting to tear her out of it. The hair shining like burnished bronze transforming the sting to the pain of needing to thread them through it. Then came the stain of peach spreading through her scrubbed skin, the pursed generosity of ruby lips, and the flash of eyes that burned like incandescent coals...

Her eyes. He should concentrate on her eyes. Focusing anywhere else would lead to consequences he hadn't charted. But her eyes arrested his spiraling reaction, put the brakes on what could develop into a runaway situation in heartbeats.

They were full of—what? Annoyance? Defiance?

That tilt of her chin, that remark confirmed both.

He could have stared at her for an hour before he forced himself to answer her, injecting his tone with an outstanding imitation of calmness. "You thought I'd send assistants to escort you to the dinner I invited you to?"

Her chin rose higher. "Were we both in the same scene an hour and a half ago? You *invited* me? In which parallel universe?"

His lips twitched. *Ya Ullah,* every irreverent word that spilled out of her mouth zinged something electric behind his sternum. Was it elation? How could it be?

She went on. "You *told* me we were having dinner. You *told* me when. And let's not forget the 'be ready' parting shot."

"And I can see that you are ready. So I assume you accepted my…suggestion, if you will."

"Oh, I certainly won't. That was no suggestion, that was a decree. As crown prince you live to issue those, don't you? Though I guess I can't blame you. I wouldn't blame a predator for making meals of other animals either."

It was no use resisting. It *was* elation. The twitch broke into a full-fledged smile. "I'm a predator now?"

She raised a matter-of-fact eyebrow. "Aren't you?"

The way he felt right now? The way he'd always felt around her? Certainly. A predator in a perpetual mating frenzy.

He wondered what cool answer she'd volley back if he told her that. Instead he said, "Aren't you going to invite me in?"

She flinched, as if he'd sprayed her with something scalding. His request horrified her that much?

The next moment he didn't have to wonder what her reaction was.

She said a clear, and clearly final, "No."

So. She wasn't inviting him in. Good call. He certainly had no idea what he was doing, inviting her to dinner, coming to her.

Oh, he'd told himself he'd extend the same courtesy to anyone he'd be working that closely with, however temporarily, that he'd had to come as he sensed she'd send anyone else away. He hadn't dwelt on why her aversion to being in his company put him out. After all, she was the woman *he'd* left for the best reasons.

But no reason felt valid anymore. He could no more stay away from her now than he could stop breathing indefinitely.

He tilted his head at her, devouring her expressions, struggling to fathom them, only her deepening color betraying the effect of his nearness.

"If I can't come in, you must come out."

"What I must do is bid you good-night and go up to bed."

Bed. Exactly where he wanted to go, too, where he wanted to sweep her, all fire and defiance, and drown in her all night.

But again he knew she hadn't thrown a suggestive word for his mind to latch on to and wander into erotic abandon.

He exhaled. "You are not going to bed, Viv." A thrill rattled through him at having her name on his tongue again after so long, the shortened form she'd told him only he had ever used. The sensation heightened at her indrawn breath, the admission of her reaction to hearing it. "We are having dinner, even if I have to order a table to be placed right in that doorway with us on either side."

"And you'd do it, too." Her lips spread in the closest thing to a real smile he'd had from her so far. "This is too funny. You standing across the threshold like a vampire denied entrance."

He smiled back at her even as he damned himself for it. "First I'm a predator, now I'm a vampire. Interesting."

Her eyes scalded down his body, before taking the same path back up to his eyes. "A cape and more pointed canines and you'd fit the bill." Before he could gauge if her eyes contained the awareness he couldn't wait to detect, they hardened. "But you can't do a thing without my consent. Or are you going to call your men to carry me out of the house?"

It *had* been awareness. And she was as angry as he was with himself for succumbing to it.

So could it be true? She *was* here for the job? Could he want her to have it? Could he be so reckless he'd have her in a position that would keep her in close proximity with him, no matter how temporarily? Wasn't that courting catastrophe?

Yes, it was. He was in no position to indulge his desires, with his every action having widespread repercussions on a whole nation, now more so than ever, with his marriage of state looming closer. As soon as a suitable bride was decided on.

That was his mind talking. His body sanctioned nothing, was punishing him as it always had for denying it its one desire. Her.

But the ugliness of the past or the volatility of the future weren't what stopped him from surrendering to its clawing demands. It was that hostile look in her eyes.

But what shook him was the need to wipe it away. The need dampened even his anger that she dared have it. Acting the wronged party? Sure she was. She had no idea he'd found out the truth.

They had been only three months into the affair he'd insisted on keeping secret, fearing the repercussions back home. He'd been recalled to Omraania but, suffering from his first infatuation at thirty-two, a man of his position and experience, he'd had no defenses against her power over him. He'd rushed to her to propose a continuation of their secret affair, this time in his kingdom.

He'd arrived at that doctors' room to overhear her saying that he meant nothing to her. She'd used those very words.

His first impulse had been to storm in, confront her, shout accusations at her. But she would have only retracted her words, and he couldn't have borne to see the mask of sincerity falling back into place. He'd left, feeling crushed by what he'd heard. She'd pursued for the same reason as every woman he'd ever known had—a bid to attain wealth and power. What he'd been about to offer her, for as long as she'd have him.

Oblivious to his eavesdropping, she'd caught up with him, had acted distraught on finding him departing. She'd clung, begged to be with him, anywhere, anyhow, whenever his duties let him. Even with what he'd learned, it had been almost impossible to conquer the temptation, his still raging hunger and emotions.

But he'd done it. He'd walked away, without one more word.

Then he'd made the mistake of taking one last look. The sight of her standing at the gate of his mansion, watching him drive away, looking devastated, would never fade from his memory.

He'd spent endless months tormented by that memory, by every nuance of her passion, the conviction of her confessions of love. He'd berated himself for forgetting what he'd heard with his own ears instead of being grateful for it. He wouldn't have been able to pay the price of keeping her in his life. Hearing the truth had saved him insupportable trouble. Had set him free.

Or so he'd tried to tell himself all these years.

Suddenly a gust of breeze threaded through his hair, seemed to pass through it to comb through hers, brushing the strands away from her face. He moved, as if he'd catch the subtle change in her expression, and the silvery rays of the dawning full moon flooded her beauty. Such beauty. All new. All hers. As he'd once been.

Memories made him surge with their flow toward her, needing to close the gap, end the separation. She muffled a gasp, receded, maintaining the distance between them.

Suddenly he was fed up with it all. Seven-years'-worth, end-of-his-tether fed up. With the doubts, the foul taste of how it had ended, the holding back. But mostly with the pretense.

A step back resumed his position across the threshold before he muttered, "All right, Viv.

Enough. Let's drop this charade. Let's stop behaving as if we don't know each other."

She leaned on the door, hands clutching its edge, as if to keep herself up. "I did no such thing."

"*Zain.* Fine. I did, then. You have to excuse me, though. Seeing you walking into the center and realizing you were my new co-head of surgery wasn't something I could get over quickly."

Her eyes widened. "You didn't know you'd hired me?"

He exhaled. "No, I didn't."

Her eyes narrowed, focusing their fire into a laserlike intensity. "So…you didn't bother to find out who Adnan picked. Then you saw me, decided not to let me see you until you got over your surprise, get on equal terms with me."

Exactly what he'd thought at the time.

She straightened from the door, recovered from his incursion into her personal space. "It's clear your surprise wasn't of the pleasant variety. No doubt your first thought was to send me back where I came from. Why didn't you?"

Surprise kicked in his gut yet again. How had she developed such insight? Or had she always had it and he'd just not seen it? Had she always been the woman he'd seen her to be today and he'd never cared to notice, lost in the conflagration of physical abandon and sensual delights?

He spread his shoulders, assuming a confrontational pose. "So you think you deserve to be sent back?"

She pulled herself to her five-foot-six height, meeting his challenge head-on. "I think no such thing. Why should I?"

"Maybe you know your past performance is against you, that I'd be justified to think your contribution would be as lacking."

She glared at him. "My past 'performance'? Where exactly? In your bed? You made it clear my 'performance' there *was* 'lacking' but what does it have to do with my professional skills?"

*Ya Ullah,* such straightforwardness. He'd never known that anyone could air everything they thought like that, hiding nothing for decorum's or social games' sake. Even if she was totally off track. She thought he'd been dissatisfied with her in bed? That was the reason she'd come up with to explain his sudden departure? He almost laughed out loud at the ludicrousness of the misconception.

He gritted his teeth on the urge to put her straight. "I was referring to your professional performance. You convinced me to make you

my research assistant back then. I don't remember much research assistance."

She folded her arms, drawing his eyes to the
voluptuousness of her breasts, before the severity
in hers dragged them up.

"I didn't intend to refer to the past, let alone go
into a dissection of it," she ground out. "But since
you brought it up, I don't remember *you* doing
much research I could assist you in."

"And we both know what distracted me," he
said abruptly. "To the point where I almost
stopped thinking of work."

"You mean me?" She gave a mirthless laugh
that still had him itching to grab her, to eat it
right out of her plump lips. "I was a very small
part of your distractions. I wasn't even that,
just a letting-off-steam outlet. What distracted
you between surgeries and the rest of your PhD
work were your remote-controlled crown
prince duties. I'm sure your research didn't
suffer, that once you left you had other assistants, whose 'performance' you approved of,
falling over themselves to fill my inadequacies
and make up for my so-called distraction. You,
on the other hand, were all my distractions.
My 'performance' did suffer during the three

months we were together, to the point where I almost quit medicine."

His heart rate built to a sustained crescendo. How could lies be so undetectable? How could every lie she'd told have the unmistakable texture of truth, of conviction? It almost made him believe them. But how could he? How could he have been all her distractions when he'd meant nothing to her?

She, on the other hand, had been all his distractions. Work and duties had ceased to matter the moment he'd set eyes on her. He'd spent his waking hours clamoring for the time he'd have her in his arms, his sleeping ones replaying it. It had been why his return had become so urgent. He'd left so many things undone, they'd accumulated into a crisis he'd been forced to return and sort out.

Now something else she'd said sent his heart thudding. "Are you implying you suffered repercussions in your job?"

Her lips twisted. "You could say that. But *I'll* be fair and say that it wasn't your doing. We have a choice in what we let people do to us. *I* let you distract me. And when…people wanted me out of their hair, they used it against me."

"But Adnan chose you after reading what he

described as an astounding résumé. Surely any setback couldn't have been serious?"

"Why couldn't it be?" She inclined her head. "You don't think I'm capable of getting back on my feet after a serious setback?"

She must know he could find out what that setback had been if he wanted to. So she must be telling the truth. This time.

But then he didn't need to check her record to answer her question. "After seeing you at work today, I think you're capable of just about anything. The range of expertise, the level of confidence and fluency you exhibited are things the best of surgeons only acquire after far longer than seven years."

Her gaze had been faltering at his admissions, surprise, something like vulnerability, even pleasure, softening it. Then his last words registered and it hardened again.

"You're assuming I was in stasis until you laid eyes on me? That I started accumulating experience and knowledge only after you left? I was a surgical resident when you met me, and I was a darned good one. I *did* approach you at first for the incredible scientific opportunity that being your research assistant would have afforded me.

It wasn't my fault that you didn't put my skills to use. I wasn't in any condition then to wonder why you didn't, but now I realize you thought I didn't have any to speak of, that you weren't using your brain when you chose me."

Which was an accurate summation of what he'd believed, what he'd done. And an unprecedented sensation clenched his guts.

Shame. At being caught out in a blind preconception, at being guilty of an injustice.

What else hadn't he seen? What else had he been guilty of? Could he have been wrong about more than that?

No. He couldn't have been. He'd *heard* her.

And even if he hadn't, he'd been insane to think he could offer her what he'd intended to. He would have been forced to choose between her and his duty sooner rather than later and he would have chosen his duty. It had all turned out for the best that he'd ended it then, and that it hadn't really hurt her.

He emptied his lungs on a heavy exhalation. "I admit I was wrong about your capabilities, and about the reason I chose you. I was also wrong when I let our relationship take a sharp detour into intimacy. Then it all went off the tracks."

She sighed. "We didn't have a relationship for it to go off the tracks. You accepted what I threw at your feet and walked away when you'd had enough." Was that bitterness? Accusation? It felt too neutral to be either. Her next words validated that. "Again, nothing I blame you for. It was my doing, as much as my setback was." So…matter-of-fact. So was this it? His final proof he'd meant nothing to her and him walking away had meant as little? He waited for more clues, She only said, "But after you left I did compensate for both lost time and the close call."

To that, he could only nod. "I had firsthand experience with the degree of success you've achieved. You've got tremendous talent and uncanny surgical and diagnostic sense, and it's clear you've backed them up with extensive training and learning."

This time there was no visible reaction to his praise. Her gaze remained steady. "I do my best. But that doesn't guarantee acceptance in this world. I applied for this job because I'm perfectly qualified for it. But with our history I had to be realistic, had to predict many outcomes. One of them was that you'd see my application and reject it out of hand."

Her analysis had the bluntness of a woman who could feel nothing. Or one who'd been too hurt she'd never risk feeling again. There *had* to be more options to explain her attitude.

"And the other possibilities?"

"That you'd be professional, decide my eligibility based on qualifications. That my name wouldn't ring a bell, gaining me fair consideration, but you'd set eyes on me and dismiss me. The last possibility was that you'd remember neither my name nor face and I'd get the benefit of a clean slate."

His guts twisted. "You thought I might not remember you?"

She shrugged one shoulder. "I'm one of countless women you've bedded. I doubt you clutter your mind with their names or faces. And, then, forgetting mine didn't seem like such a leap. It would have been just a step up from knowing nothing about me."

The need to refute her statement boiled his blood. She hadn't been a woman he'd "bedded," not one in hundreds. He'd cared about her. He'd thought he'd *loved* her. He *had*...

"I know a lot about you," he bit off. "Where

you went to medical school, where you spent your early residency…"

He stopped. *He knew nothing about her beyond that.*

At least, he knew no facts. He knew everything about her preferences—in food, music, reading, entertainment, sports and a thousand things from toothpaste brand to the number of spoons of sugar in various beverages. He knew in intimate detail how she liked to be touched, where, what made her whimper, what made her beg, what gave her so much pleasure she wept with it. But he knew nothing about her life, her past. He wasn't even sure of her age.

She gestured at him. "See? But as it turned out, all my projections came to nothing. You delegated this decision to Adnan, and found out he'd chosen me minutes before we met. Now I have more projections. About why you didn't send me away. You're either intrigued, or you're being professional. I'd go for choice A."

Again this ultra-accurate fathoming of his mind!

She gave him no respite. "What I don't get is why the curiosity now. When you lost interest so totally before you didn't think you owed me a goodbye you'd give a passing acquaintance."

*I owed you nothing. I believed in you, in your love. But you didn't deserve my faith, certainly nothing else...*

He grated, "We've examined my actions and theorized on my motives, past and present, closely enough, don't you think? How about we turn to yours?"

Her gaze emptied. "There's nothing to examine. In the past I was just too obvious. Right now I'm here to work."

"If you are, why do you find it hard to believe that work is what I'm also considering and nothing else?"

She gave a conceding nod. "So you're above abusing your power and playing games. Good for you. I, on the other hand, am human. And I've reached the limits of my endurance. Will you, please, forget about this dinner and let me go to sleep?"

# CHAPTER FOUR

GHALEB STARED at Viv. How untrue everything she'd said was.

He wasn't above abusing his power, if it would get him more of her, if it would soothe the resurrected and growing chaos.

And she was certainly more than human. A vision come to life.

If he'd been given the power to create the female that encompassed his unreasonable demands and far-fetched fantasies, the resulting creation would be her. Which was strange since he'd thought the same of her younger self, a very different physical specimen to the creature standing before him now.

So what did it mean? That Viv would fulfill his fantasies, no matter what she looked like? That his tastes changed with the changes in her, so that she remained his ideal?

He'd suspected as much since he'd left her,

when he'd been denied pleasure in another's touch, appreciation or even tolerance of any other form of beauty.

So was he forever doomed to find no satisfaction except with her, in her? Was the call of her essence the only thing that would access the male in him, send him raging in uncontainable passion?

Why did it have to be her? When she felt nothing in return?

But it was her. And she was here. And she was so much more than he'd ever dreamed. He'd been wrong about her. Up to a point. If she was here for the job, he owed it to her to give it to her. And he should take her, for as long as he was still free to. He didn't know when his freedom would end, should seize the moment. He had no idea what would precipitate the end this time. Finding a replacement. The scheduling of his marriage. Having enough of her.

Yes, he *had* to have enough of her. If he was to exorcise her, he had to reignite the affair he'd felt incomplete for ending while everything in him had raged for more. He'd get more. He'd give her what she wanted, too, whatever it was, in full.

Something clicked in his mind, the decision

and his conviction of its necessity dissipating his upheaval.

His body relaxed, his smile spread, his voice teasing when he murmured, "You're not telling me the whole truth."

She blinked, bewilderment flooding her eyes as she noted the change that had come over him, before something else flared there. Panic? Surely not. What was there for her to fear? Him? No way.

He watched her closely, but it was gone, whatever he'd seen.

She finally rasped, "What are you talking about now?"

He shrugged. "The part about being human. I know of no human who can travel across the world, then, without dropping a beat, plunge into ten demanding surgeries, then not only remain on her feet afterwards but talk circles around me."

Both eyebrows rose. "Oh, and who is the inhuman creature who made me do all that, I wonder?"

He laughed, loving every word she uttered, loving engaging in verbal battles with her now that his mind was made up, now that he'd given himself license to pursue this, pursue her. They'd never talked much during their white-hot liaison, and he was beginning to realize what he'd missed, what he couldn't get enough of now.

"It was all a plan to out you. And if I didn't discover your secret by all of the above, this..." he made a gesture descriptive of the way they stood on opposite sides of the door "...is proof positive. I certainly know of no human who can make me stand on a doorstep like a rejected salesman."

She wrinkled her nose at him. He didn't know how he remained where he was. "Why don't you say it's you who's making me stand on my doorstep, answering questions like some murder suspect?"

"I didn't start asking questions. In fact, I don't remember how all this started."

"What a convenient memory you have. Well, *I* do...it was all you," she insisted. "And it's incredible that I was able to withstand your interrogation, what with a combination of jet lag, exhaustion and hypoglycemia."

"And yet you refuse to let me replenish you."

"What I need to replenish me is a load of highly accessible calories followed by an eight-hour sleep."

He flattened his palm against the door frame, assuming a relaxed pose, letting the inches he allowed himself closer heighten the impact of his next words. "But I am offering so much better than that. A calorie-laden aperitif in the back of my limo, a rejuvenating hour's nap until we arrive at our destination, then a meal that will make your first day in Omraania live on in your memory."

A few moments passed before a soft sound caught in her throat and a stiff movement reestablished their distance as she gave him a ridiculing look. "It's already memorable, never fear."

He made up for her distancing attempt, his expression draining of lightness as convincing her to step over that threshold metamorphosed from need to necessity. "It's been so for being full of exhaustion and tension and echoes of memories that should be left in the past. You're here and I'm glad you're here…"

She gave a sarcastic laugh. "Are you now?"

"*I am.*" The intensity in those two words shocked him as much as it did her. He leashed what he could of it. "It's different now and you know it. You feel it. You felt it the moment we laid eyes on each other again. *We're* different. The people we were seven years ago wouldn't have spent ten hours saving lives together, wouldn't have had the conversation we just had, shared that level of frankness. Let us get to know each other all over again, without holding the past against each other. Let me take you to dinner, Viv. Let me wipe the bad taste away, replace it with all the delights my kingdom has to offer."

Her face lost its cynical expression as he spoke, hesitation replacing it. Was that a touch of vulnerability, too? Was she afraid to let down her guard around him? Could it be she'd been hurt when he'd left her? Had him walking away made her realize he'd meant something to her after all?

But what was the use of wondering? He should take his own advice, leave the past in the past, where it was inaccessible, insignificant. It was in the here and now that he was certain.

He wanted her again. Far more than ever before.

And she wanted him. He may not have meant anything to her emotionally but her desire had never been in doubt. He'd make her remember how much she'd craved him, make her beg for what he'd once given her. Only then would he take her. And keep taking her.

He pressed his advantage, his voice roughened with his effort to suppress his urgency. "Say yes, Viv."

His husky request brought spectacular color storming over features turned transparent, letting him read each nuance of her conflict as she went from hesitant to reluctant to capitulating.

She finally exhaled. "Oh, all right. But don't blame anyone but yourself if I fall asleep the moment I sit down and you can't wake me up before morning."

He laughed. "Oh, I know how to wake you up."

Her softened gaze sharpened. She thought he was referring to the many times he'd woken her up using arousal, pleasure, even possession. And she didn't like it. In fact, she was outraged.

Before she singed him with her displeasure, he hastened to add, "I promise tickling will only be a last resort."

In answer, she looked at him with something akin to reproach in those magnificent golden eyes.

Just a second before he lost all control, snatched her out of that damned doorway, she exhaled again, let her shoulders sag.

Then she crossed over the threshold.

Viv jerked awake.

Not to tickling. Or to anything disturbing. It was the stillness, the steadiness of the rhythm permeating her, the warmth and security enveloping her that snatched her from the depths.

It was the hot, spicy virility that filled her lungs when she gasped that crashed her back into her body. *Ghaleb.*

He was the warmth and security surrounding her, the rhythm rocking her that of his heart, the heart her head rested over.

She was in his arms. Half lying over him.

The urge to come fully over him was what spilled her back onto the seat and as far away from him as possible. He remained unmoving. But she knew he was awake. And watching her.

She looked everywhere but at him, her dazed gaze slamming around the interior of his limo, a duplicate of the one he'd allocated for her use. He really was giving her the royal treatment.

She stated the obvious. "We're not moving."

"We arrived some time ago."

She looked at him then immediately wished she hadn't.

Her heartbeats scattered at the sight of him brooding at her from the far side of the seat, all slashed bones and fathomless eyes, his jacket open, his body spread in the same position she'd found so comfortable to drape herself over.

"Uh…how long is 'some time'?" She winced when she heard the huskiness in her voice, hoped he'd think it sleep-induced.

"An hour…or so."

"What would 'or so' be on a clock?"

"Another hour."

She sagged against her door. "You mean I've been asleep all over you for two hours?"

The intensity in his gaze began to melt, becoming more distressing. "The all-over-me part was half of that. The overall sleeping time was around three hours since you did fulfill your threat and lost consciousness the moment you hit the seat and it took over an hour to arrive here."

"Why didn't you *wake* me?"

His smile broke out, indulgent, knocking a dozen heartbeats out of place. "I tried. I discovered you are tickle-proof now."

"You didn't try, did you?" she accused.

He shrugged, and confessed, "I didn't have the heart. You needed the rest."

"Gee, really? Where have I heard that before, I wonder?"

His smile grew unrepentant. "You're clearly rested now."

And she was. As if she'd slept those eight hours

she'd thought she'd needed after the last grueling forty-eight.

"I sleep a maximum of five hours," she admitted. "So three is almost a full night's sleep. And you make a great mattress."

She bit her tongue, horrified at what kept spilling from her mouth around him. First the true confessions at her door, now this. No wonder he was looking at her as if she'd grown a second head...

Suddenly his laughter boomed. Guffaw after guffaw of cruelly masculine, unrestrained mirth. Her jaw dropped open.

*She'd never heard him laugh like that.*

She'd never heard him laugh at all. Their liaison had been all about raging desire and sensual abandon. She hadn't been in any mental state to be witty or to even feel playful. She'd never teased him or joked with him. Besides agreeing to everything he'd said and telling him in every way she could think of how happy she'd been to be with him, she hadn't talked much, afraid she'd say something stupid or out of place or boring, or just do something that would make him walk away. He'd walked away anyway.

It had taken her father to teach her that seeking

anyone's approval and affection at the expense of her pride or common sense led only to heartache and misery. She'd trained herself never to suppress her doubts or instincts, her opinions or responses. She'd resolved to build the strongest self she could and remain true to it come what may.

It seemed that resolution was paying off, bigtime. It had won her many smiles today. Now *this.*

She stared at him as he wiped away tears. "*Ya Ullah, ya* Viv...I don't remember when I last laughed like that. If I ever laughed like that."

Resigned she'd have to live with arrhythmia with him around, she smirked. "So glad to be of service. Maybe if I don't fit your co-head position, I can apply for the court clown's."

The guffaws that had settled into rumbles erupted again, until he started to choke.

She rolled her eyes. "Great. Seems I'll manage to kill Omraania's crown prince on my first day. It sure won't make it any better when I tell your people that you died happy."

"*Er-ruhmuh ya,* Viv... Mercy..."

She opened her mouth and a large, gentle hand closed it for her. The feel of his skin on her lips paralyzed her. "I'm not ready to die...happy or otherwise. Uh-uh…" he panted, misinterpreting her squirming efforts to free herself before she was tempted to bury her lips into his palm. "Not one more word."

Then his hand was off her lips and he was outside the car and reaching back for her, had her out in seconds.

The cool breeze hit her after the heat emanating from him and the situation. She shuddered. His arms went around her at once, loose, undemanding, yet offering rocklike support and the insulation of his formidable body.

Her balance lost, her fingers dug into his arms through the amazingly soft fabric of his jacket as she steadied herself.

Was this lightheartedness a new enhancement to his character? Could someone grow a sense of humor? Or had he always been like that and she'd been too lovesick to notice? Or had he never thought that she warranted showing her this side of him?

She waited for the bitterness to well up. It didn't. Instead, unknown ease spread. No matter what the reasons had been, he'd been right. There was nothing to be gained by dredging up the past. It was dead and gone. The present was very much alive. And so much better than anything she could have dreamed of.

She'd never expected the day would come when they'd laugh together like that. And whether it was hypoglycemia or jet lag, her own weakness or his own type of mind control, all she found feasible, or even possible, was to indulge in the unexpected gift of smashed preconceptions, plunge into the moment.

But now that the humorous moments had passed, what had felt like an exorcism of all the ugliness and bitterness of the past, they stood staring at each other, uncertain how to proceed.

Then he spread one arm in a theatrical gesture. "Before *I'm* held responsible for starving you to death, shall we?"

Her gaze followed the direction he indicated, and she gasped.

They stood at the edge of an expansive court-yard leading to a dozen steps flanked by arches and columns, giving onto what looked like a castle that had been transported from the era of the genies and their magical lamps.

She gaped until his hand engulfed hers and tugged, starting her legs toward the central arch, imparting a feel of walking into an ancient temple.

She stared ahead as they approached massive wooden doors decorated in gleaming copperwork. Footmen dressed in white materialized like ghosts, hastening to open them wide.

The moment they stepped inside, heavy fumes of incense hit her. Her step wobbled.

"The *ood* scent upsets you?" His grip tightened, taking most of her weight, his eyes alarmed.

"Yes… No…" she gasped as more of the sweet-spicy scent permeated her lungs. "It's lovely…just a bit too heavy."

He snapped his eyes around to the man who seemed to be a sort of maître d' in amazingly ornate garb. *"Ma benreed bokhoor."*

The man snapped his fingers and a dozen men appeared to remove the filigree incense burners hanging from the ceiling while others ran inside, no doubt to purge the rest of the place.

"Hey, not all of them!" she croaked.

Ghaleb addressed the man again. *"Etrok wahed bed'dakhel."* He looked down at her, his gaze brimming with solicitude. "Better now?"

She gulped, nodded. He looked at her for a moment before he inclined his head, inviting her to walk on. She did, following the man who led the way into the dimly lit interior through damask drapes woven with elaborate designs. The feeling of stepping back centuries in time intensified as they entered a ballroom-sized circular hall with a soaring ceiling and lit with dozens of hand-crafted copper lanterns hanging from  thick brass chains. The only incense burner left was an urn in the middle of the floor with *ood* fumes swirling up from glowing coals.

The place had to be an exclusive restaurant, clearly reserved for them. The seating was on very low couches lining the whitewashed walls, upholstered in arabesque-patterned brocade, with low, round mahogany tables in front of them, the rest of the seating being throw cushions littering a floor covered in handwoven carpets.

"You should have told me we were having dinner in the past," she mumbled as he led her to a couch by an arabesque veranda door thrown open to let in the crisp desert breeze.

He gave her a smile that made her stumble. His grip went to her elbow, supporting her as his voice slithered across her nerves. "I hope my choice of era meets with your approval?"

She marveled at how he was on the exact wave-length as she was, ready with a comeback.

"Perfect. I just wonder where you parked your flying carpet."

His smile grew crooked. "Right by my time machine, of course."

She gave in to the temptation, stuck her tongue out at him.

He threw his head back and let out a gusty laugh and she almost collapsed on the couch.

His laughter came to an abrupt end as he came down beside her in alarm. "Are you all right?"

"Food," she gasped. "Lots of it. Quick."

His smile was one of relief. And devilment. Then he raised his hand in an imperious gesture, and a battalion of waiters came forward bearing a feast.

Ghaleb watched the half-prone Viv as she chased a long, thick finger of *balah esh-Sham* around her plate. She picked it up, scrunched into the golden crispy exterior to the doughy syrup-laden interior and moaned in enjoyment. He almost moaned, too.

She licked her fingers, sighed. "This is beyond sinful. Not to mention catastrophic. I feel my dimensions changing already."

His eyes traveled over her, reveling in the

changes maturity had given her. "You can afford a few inches."

"Oh, no, I can't." She tried to sit up, gave up and resumed her pose. "I found an old pair of pants as I packed and made the mistake of trying them on. They didn't clear my calves."

"You were too slim in the past. You're perfect now."

Color rushed to her face as she reached for another piece. "And you must be getting on in age and in need of glasses."

He laughed. It was all so unbelievable. That she made him laugh like that, when they'd never laughed together before, when he hadn't known he was capable of responding so easily, so uninhibitedly. And for it to be with her of all people. But then again he'd never lost his inhibitions with anyone else.

It was also strange that his praise made her blush. The woman he'd known in extreme intimacy. The woman who'd dueled with him today, winning almost every challenge, who seemed incapable of being cornered or embarrassed. It was strange, seeing her blush at all. She'd been so tanned before he'd never had the pleasure.

She looked, felt so changed, affected him so

differently. Which further proved his theory that it was her, not the way she looked or behaved, that commanded his responses. And now hunger for food had been satisfied, now the enchanted evening had flowed with his delight in her company, another kind of hunger raged in him.

He sipped his cardamom coffee, amazed again at how the day had started, how a day could change everything.

And everything had changed. He had brought her here still unwilling to acknowledge any genuine pleasure in her company. But the pleasure had risen until he'd succumbed to the exhilaration of rediscovering her. Or discovering the new woman she'd become. His earlier convictions and intentions were fading, along with the anger and bitterness that had been poisoning him all those years.

The new Viv was infusing the antidote into his blood, and for the first time he even considered things might not have been as bad as he'd thought. All he had against her were half a dozen words. Words that might have had an acceptable explanation.

Even if there wasn't one, he felt he could put it behind him. This was a new beginning, in a new life. They *were* different now, and the past no longer mattered. He'd said that to gain her acceptance to come here with him, to work out her game. But he more and more believed it himself now.

He must have her in Omraania indefinitely. As he'd wanted seven years ago. An open-ended contract would achieve that. And as she stayed here, near, working with him, he'd find a way, to safeguard against—

"What's that?"

His eyes snapped to where she was pointing. "What's what?"

"The light outside."

"What do you think it is?" he teased. "The floodlights of the helicopter sent to search for me? It's dawn, of course."

Her eyes went round. "Dawn? No way!"

His eyes roamed hungrily over her. "Yet it did find a way. The sun is tenacious like that. It also has a knack of making a speedy appearance when one doesn't want the night to end."

She nodded, in a daze. "Yeah. Oh, wow. I can't believe we've been here for over five hours." Suddenly something akin to panic flared in her eyes. "I have to go back at once!"

He leaned over, pressed her gently back on the

couch. "Relax, we don't have to rush on account of anything."

"But we have work in the morning…make that in a couple of hours!" she exclaimed as she scooted over the couch and sat up.

He sat up, too, unwilling to end the magical time. "Work won't come to a grinding halt if we take much-deserved time off. And then you weren't supposed to be working on your first day. And yes, I am the beast who made you work fresh off the plane. Now you'll take as many days as you want to rest, to get your bearings. When you've settled in, I'll take you to explore the treasures that Jobail and the rest of Omraania have to offer."

She frowned. "And where does work fit into this?"

He shrugged. "Work won't go anywhere. You proved you're all I need to share my medical position, even to take it over single-handedly, but holding down the fort alone a little longer won't kill me. The most important thing now is for you to settle in, get acquainted with the country, the people, the language…"

She cut across him. "You're talking about things that would take months."

His lips spread at the idea of leisurely months

of guiding her through his land, of exploring her.
"Then take months."

"But I'm here for only two months."

He tensed. "Why only two months?"

"That's the length of the contract Adnan—
you—offered me."

He relaxed again. "That was until I made up
my mind whether to make the position permanent or whether to look for someone else. And
I've already made my mind up. I'm offering you
an open-ended contract now."

"But if you'd made any of this clear, I wouldn't
have applied!" she exclaimed. "I thought this
was a strictly temporary position. Two months is
the leave I have from my job. And then there's
S—" She turned her eyes away. "I'm sorry. I
can't take up your offer."

He felt everything toppling in his mind like a
house of cards.

"What is this, Viv?" he grated, disappointment
crashing into his system. "You got me to admit
how much I need you and now you're—what?
Bargaining for more money and benefits?"

The moment the words were out, even before
all animation drained from her face, he realized
he'd made an irretrievable mistake.

*Ya Ullah,* what he'd do for a time machine to rewind to that magical mood. "Viv, I didn't mean—"

"I did." She heaved up to her feet, her eyes cold. "I'm here for two months. If your offer is to take it or leave it, you'll have to terminate my contract now. Otherwise I'll fill the slot you need filled until you find someone else. Meanwhile, save your offers of more money and benefits. You're already paying me a salary I can retire on. Now take me back."

# CHAPTER FIVE

HE'D TAKEN HER BACK. In silence.

She'd gone to work only three hours after he'd dropped her at her villa, to work her way through another grueling day.

Then, during the past week, she'd showed up to work at 8 a.m. sharp every day, rarely leaving before midnight.

But along the way her resolve to treat him as non-existent kept slipping. He discovered her sense of duty bordered on the obsessive, that nothing made her lose all reserve more than being in her element, being needed, depended on. He hadn't been above using the knowledge to make it impossible for her to ignore him, compelling her input, her interaction.

But that had ceased to be a manipulation technique almost from the start, counting on her becoming a necessity.

No matter how temporary she kept insisting

her presence would be, she threw herself into the thick of things with energy and zeal, doing everything with the utmost involvement and dedication, treating everyone with the utmost care and consideration.

Her popularity as a person swept the center and the story of her first day on the job, followed by fresh accounts every day, had established her reputation as an imperturbable OR leader, someone on a par with Ghaleb. Every one of his staff had managed to have a private moment with him to commend his find.

And everyone, starting with her, was wondering what he was doing, spending even more time in the center, partnering her in the OR, instead of leaving her to the job he'd hired her to do and using the time she'd freed for him to tend to other responsibilities.

To everyone he made it clear he wasn't to be questioned. To her he only said all was going to plan. To himself he admitted he couldn't do anything else. He had to be near her.

He slept less so he wouldn't neglect his other duties totally but, like in the past, he planned his days around being with her, this time experiencing her to the full. Every hour made him realize how the too-fast-and-furious plunge into sexual intimacy had stunted his recognition of her different facets, while making him recognize the years had brought out the best in her, had changed his priorities and mindset so he could appreciate every basic trait, each new enhancement. Every day the past, even its good parts, seemed as if it had happened to someone else.

Not that she let him near outside work. She refused his apology or any offers of personal time again.

His only solace was once they hit the OR she melded with him in the intensity of interaction, poured out her skills and intuition, her eyes and senses and actions meshing with his in the depth of decision-making, in the execution of one surgery after another. During today's list their fusion into one ultra-efficient whole had reached its zenith during a horrific complication.

Now they'd reached the last surgery on their list and, as he'd felt each day of the last week, he felt drunk with exhilaration at the incredible rapport and synergy between them, what he'd never thought to share with another, let alone her.

No, he was beyond drunk. He was addicted. It

seemed the only highs capable of addicting him had to involve her…

"History?"

Viv's question brought him out of his fugue, made him realize he'd been staring at her. She was looking down at the woman being prepped on table.

He'd taken a look at their patient's file minutes ago. He started to answer her, but she looked up, her eyes bypassing him and zeroing in on Aneesah. He clamped his lips beneath his mask.

Another episode of ignoring him or just pursuing her teaching role?

He almost winced as Aneesah's dark eyes flashed in pleasure at the attention and the acknowledgment Viv had been lavishing on her. He knew how she felt. How incredible it was to be in Viv's focus. The focus he felt she'd banished him from yet again.

Giving himself a mental kick, he murmured orders to his team smoothing the transition between the case they'd finished and the one they were about to begin, but most of his attention was on the scene unfolding between Viv and Aneesah.

"Es-Sayedah Lateefah presented at 3 a.m. with severe abdominal pain, nausea and vomiting,"

Aneesah said in the tone of a student showing off her prowess to her teacher. "After examination, my provisional diagnosis was acute exacerbation of chronic calcular cholecytitis."

"You admitted her?" Viv asked. Aneesah nodded. "Since it's almost midnight, I salute your stamina, Dr. Aneesah."

Aneesah's eyes glowed. Another resident mumbled something about Aneesah belonging to an alien race. Someone else suppressed a yawn, sending a chain reaction of yawns throughout the OR.

"It's our last surgery, people," Ghaleb said. "Let's postpone all those bedtime noises a bit longer."

A merry if sheepish ripple spread at his calm words. Ghaleb watched everyone making a visible effort to perk up, feeling sorry for them. Keeping up with Aneesah and Viv, two ladies who seemed tireless, was taking its toll on everyone. He, on the other hand, had enough hormones, stress and every other kind, gushing in his system that he doubted he'd register fatigue if he stayed on his feet and in surgery for three days on end.

"Rather than belonging to a sturdier species," Viv said lightly, indirectly answering Lo'ai, who now had his belligerent if covetous eyes pinned on Aneesah, "Dr. Aneesah does a few things we should all be doing. I advise everyone to emulate her dietary and exercise habits and relaxation techniques."

Ghaleb couldn't have agreed more. Aneesah was disciplined, no-nonsense and driven. Things she had in common with Viv, explaining the understanding and appreciation that connected the two women. Aneesah was also getting a huge kick out of having a woman in a position on par with her head of surgery who happened to be her crown prince. It gave her hope for the future. A hope he believed would come to pass, with her showing promise as a surgeon and many leadership qualities and people skills. He'd make certain of it.

"Dr. Hashim, before I miss the chance again," Viv said, a smile permeating her voice, her gaze, the smile he'd do anything to see, the one she was now bestowing on Hashim, "Let me thank you for always bringing our patients sedated to the OR."

"Surely that's nothing to thank me for, Dr. Vivienne!" Hashim exclaimed, surprised but fluttering under Viv's praise, his eyes unable to hide his immense attraction.

Viv shook her head. "Oh, it is. If you think it's what all anesthetists do, to save everyone, especially the patients' anxiety and unpleasantness, let me tell you it's a merciful practice that's more overlooked than not."

Ghaleb knew what she was doing. She periodically chose someone in the OR, praised a trait they considered nothing worth praising and drawing everyone's attention to what she considered good practice without criticizing anyone or giving outright directions.

This was nothing like his own direct methods of getting the best out of his people, but it was as effective, if not more so. Her subtle ways were working, his team becoming even more efficient, since each time she'd been spot on. She was spot on now.

He still gritted his teeth against the urge to haul Dr. Hashim out of the anesthesia station and hurl him out of the OR.

Thankfully, she returned her gaze from the man back to Aneesah. "Investigations?"

"Ultrasound showed three gallstones, around two centimeters each." Aneesah motioned urgently to one of the nurses, who came forward with the patient's documents for Viv to peruse.

Viv gave her an appreciative glance before turning her eyes on them.

After a few moments Viv thanked the nurse, walked around the table, stopped a foot from Ghaleb, showing everyone her back.

He blinked into her upturned eyes. He'd been resigned she wouldn't acknowledge him again tonight so her approach stymied him.

"We have an obese, diabetic patient..." Her murmur was so low he had to strain to hear her. "A perfect candidate for laparoscopic surgery and the worst possible for open abdominal surgery. Any reason you scheduled her for the open route?"

*B'hag'gejaheem*—hell, she'd only approached him to attack him!

At least his surgical decision. She did it for his ears only, careful not to let anyone pick up on any dissension, but her eyes were taking him apart and—*ya Ullah*—*was* there any situation where she wouldn't inflame him?

His lips twisted. If he were in better shape, he would have found her periodic attempts to reestablish hostilities after her persistent lapses into the fluency of their communication amusing. He only found them disheartening, maddening. Unbearably arousing.

He leaned closer, felt her warmth and femininity permeating his lungs even over the overpowering OR scents. Her pupils expanded like black holes engulfing the suns of her eyes, sending a thrill storming through him at the involuntary confession he saw there.

Satisfied that whatever coldness she exhibited was only a superficial layer, he lowered his head to hers, keeping his voice as low as hers had been. "There's a simple answer to that. I *didn't* schedule her. Contrary to what everyone believes, I'm not everywhere. Es-Sayedah Lateefah was admitted, examined and scheduled for surgery by your star student."

"Oh…" Comprehension flooded her eyes, making him want to press his advantage, have her make up for her presumption by reinitiating interaction. But when mortification followed it, he wanted only to snatch her in his arms and erase the troubled expression, spare her the distress.

He moved closer, felt her groping for his support, offered it urgently. "You don't need to call her on it. I'll do it."

He kept her eyes captive as hesitation softened them, willing her to agree. Instead, they firmed up with decision. "No, I will. I'm occupying the same position as you, with the same powers and responsibilities, right? I get to deal with the same discomforts."

"You don't have to," he insisted.

She only said, "I do." Then she walked back to her former position, looked over at Aneesah. "You were going to do this surgery yourself, weren't you?"

Aneesah, sensing something wrong, started defensively, "As a second-year resident I'm allowed to do certain surgeries alone."

"I was going to assist her." That was Lo'ai, who'd commented earlier on Aneesah's humanity.

Seeing how he'd jumped to her assistance when he wasn't sure yet if she was in trouble, if he'd land himself in it himself, it seemed his earlier attitude had been caused either by languishing in unrequited passion or being the victim of his lady's cold shoulder. In either case, Ghaleb could sympathize with him.

But it seemed Lo'ai's selfless gesture had worked wonders. Aneesah now shot him a look full of gratitude and promise, before turning apprehensive eyes on Ghaleb and Viv.

Ghaleb watched Viv with gritted teeth, hating it that she hadn't let him spare her when he could have handled the situation much more easily. But he *would* intervene if he thought it necessary.

"You scheduled her for open abdominal surgery?" Viv asked.

"Y-yes," Aneesah said, her eyes growing frantic. "All senior surgeons had full lists, leaving only me and Lo'ai available. And though I know laparoscopic surgery is indicated for her, neither of us is qualified enough for it without supervision yet."

"So when I and Dr. Ghaleb expanded our list and included her," Viv said, "you had no time to change your schedule for her."

Aneesah nodded, beyond mortified now.

"I commend you and Dr. Lo'ai on your decision." At that unexpected declaration, everyone, starting with Ghaleb, gaped at Viv. "You knew she had to be operated on within twenty-four hours and opted for a procedure you've perfected. Many overzealous residents would have opted for the indicated procedure they're inexperienced in rather than brave a harder surgery they're competent to do."

Lo'ai visibly shuddered with relief. Aneesah looked as if she'd faint. Ghaleb wanted to grab Viv and kiss her until *she* did.

She'd defused that situation far better than he

would have done, saw a positive angle he hadn't, and had come out with the paradox of an endorsement that was also a lesson.

And she wasn't finished. "Next time *do* impose on someone with the needed experience. *This* time it all turned out for everyone's benefit. Es-Sayedah Lateefah will have her indicated surgery, while you'll have two specialists in minimally invasive surgery giving you a demonstration. On the next list you'll repeat what you see under my supervision. I also want all you residents to report on the areas you're not experienced in so we can schedule you for intensive training to fill the gaps."

Aneesah nodded so eagerly a chuckle ran through the OR.

Ghaleb let out a breath he hadn't known he'd been holding and moved forward, bringing all eyes back to him. He'd been keeping to the background on purpose, letting Viv occupy center stage, establish her power with the people she'd lead. Now that she'd achieved another spectacular success on all fronts, it was time to wrap the day up.

"All right," he said, "let's start the demonstration."

In minutes, all needed equipment for the surgery was ready and Hashim gave the go-ahead.

Viv looked at Ghaleb. "Where do you want me?"

She meant at which of the ports they were going to access the patient's abdomen from. But if she kept asking that question, that way, he'd end up telling her where he wanted her, and how.

He cleared his throat, his head. "Take the two upper ports." She complied at once as he performed a small incision above the umbilicus, produced the carbon dioxide tube nozzle and inflated the abdomen then introduced the laparoscope. "Camera in. You're on."

Without looking at him, Viv made two tiny incisions, introduced the two blunt forceps they'd use to maneuver their way to the gall bladder, all the time describing every action taken, explaining the anatomy, the instruments, making sure the recorded surgery would be a valuable teaching tool.

Her eyes swung up. "You want to do the honors?"

"You go ahead," he murmured.

She gave him a look that said, *Still testing me?*

Ghaleb hoped his eyes told her what he now thought beyond a shadow of doubt. *I just love to see you at work.*

With eyes not betraying if his meaning had

reached her, Viv started dissecting the inflamed gallbladder from the liver's surface, watching her actions on the monitor, along with everyone else.

"Dr. Ghaleb…" she said, the "Dr." still jarring him every time she said it. "The gallbladder is too distended. Please, drain some bile so I can apply a clamp grasper."

He did and she continued describing their actions, their hands a blur of synchronized efficiency. They no longer asked the other for anything, certain of each other's needs and next moves and taking the necessary actions as if they shared the same mind.

"Now Dr. Ghaleb is inserting a soft drain," Viv told their audience, "to ensure all wash-out fluid is removed early in the postoperative period. Now I'll hand the gallbladder from forceps to clawed grabber, then pull it out. You'll have to be very careful here to avoid rupturing it while pulling."

Once it was out, Ghaleb removed the ports one after the other, ensured hemostasis then closed.

"Twenty-five minutes!" Lo'ai exclaimed. "That has to be some record, Dr. Vivienne."

Ghaleb's lips twitched at Lo'ai's awe, which was shared by everyone else in the OR.

Just a week ago he'd been their surgical

epitome. Now they credited only Viv with the speed and efficiency of the procedure. They must be thinking he'd never done it that fast, that the current speed was her doing. He could argue the result had stemmed from their collaboration, that he'd never been that fast because he'd never had her to work with, that she wouldn't be as fast without him. He wouldn't, though. He wanted her to receive her full due.

"It is," he agreed, looked at Viv to share the pleasure of a job well done. In answer, she walked away. He quelled the surge of frustration to call out his usual salute after a successful list. "Great job all round, everyone. Thank you."

Everyone said something appreciative back. He only had eyes for Viv as he followed her to the soiled room. She avoided looking at him, got rid of her scrubs and rushed out.

He caught up with her as she left, ready to flee the center. He blocked her escape route.

"Don't you think you've punished me enough?" he drawled.

She exhaled, let her shoulders droop with exhaustion. "It's been a long day, Ghaleb. How about I tackle this riddle tomorrow?"

His hands burned, needing to touch her, to

soothe the tiredness from her face, massage it from her shoulders. "I won't keep you long. Accept my apology. Let's move past this."

"I fully appreciate that an apology from you is a once-in-a-lifetime thing, but why should you care if I accept it or not? Whatever I feel doesn't affect my performance."

"I can see that," he ground out. "And I do care. I insulted you when I implied you were being manipulative."

Her lips twisted. "Come to think of it, holding out for more money and benefits once I knew how needed I was, when you were making a new offer, can't be called manipulation but negotiation. I'm sure you're constantly involved in such bargaining, from job offers to state matters. So we can say what you said wasn't an insult or an implication of anything but just the chagrin of a boss who thought he'd get his way on the same terms, his annoyance with the employee who got the better of him, cornering him into improving his offer. A businesslike response, really, one I've had before. So no apology needed. How's that?"

*B'Ellahi.* Would she ever stop surprising him?

A smile tugged at his lips. He was still undecided if this response was what he was after. "That's great of you, to let me off the hook. But no matter what you really think, I want you to negotiate any increase in money and benefits, and I mean any. I'm setting no limit. Shall I set up a meeting with Adnan for you to iron out particulars?"

"No," she said, her voice and face the very sound and image of finality. "Thanks for the offer, but it's still no, thanks. This time without any angst, rest assured. It's very flattering you think I warrant all that. Phew, a year of this unlimited generosity and I'd buy my own island to retire on. But at least now you know I'm not bargaining for more, as I'm turning down carte blanche."

He fisted his hands so he wouldn't grab her by the shoulders and shake her. He vented his frustration in a hiss. "Why are you turning it down, Viv?"

"Because I have a life to go back to."

His heart gave one massive detonation before stampeding into high gear, all his muscles tensing until they hurt.

Jealousy. Acrid, foul. Something he'd never felt on her account. Which was stupid to feel. She must have had many lovers since him. As he had since her. If he could call the empty disappointments he'd had since her having lovers.

Did she have one now? Was that why she was

resisting him so implacably? Did that man mean something to her? Something so big she owed him her fidelity?

Did she love him, like she hadn't loved *him?*

"You have someone waiting for you?" His voice was gruff with a dozen lacerating emotions.

"If you mean a man, no," she said, so easily, so readily that all his tension drained so quickly he felt dizzy. She was telling the truth. He knew it. "I have my job, my house, my country. My life as I said. I had no plans to leave it except temporarily."

He took another step closer, almost plastering her back to the wall. "Plans change. You can make your life here."

A step sideways reestablished their distance. "No, I can't."

"Because of our past?"

"Because of our present. I came here to stand in *for* you, not to work *with* you. Certainly not to have dinners and lunch and coffee breaks and generally spend every waking moment with you."

He remained where he was with a supreme effort, everything screaming for him to drag her into her quarters, devour her, arouse her, pleasure her until she submitted.

But this was a negotiation he couldn't resolve that way. He wanted her to see there were more than stolen times with him for her here, that a fulfilling career and a full life he'd make sure she would have could be hers if she took up his offer.

"So you came with expectations and preconceptions," he started, infusing his tone with a calmness he was far from feeling. "I would have let mine dictate my actions, too, wouldn't have hired you if I'd known it was you. There, I admitted I would have let the past blind me to your eligibility. But look at me now. I'm looking at your reality, not heeding my prejudices. I am ready to do whatever it takes to keep you here indefinitely. Things change, Viv. Things *have* changed."

"Some things, yes. Others, those that matter, can't ever change." Before he could work out her meaning, let alone think of an answer, she sidestepped him and hurried away, tossing over her shoulder, "See you tomorrow."

Apart from grabbing her and forcing her to stay, he could do nothing but watch her go.

But what had she meant by the things that mattered? His status? His impending betrothal? Did she know about that? Did it matter to her? In the past nothing had. So did she want him, but wouldn't have him on the same terms as before? Did that mean this time she might be developing feelings for him? Did he even want her to?

He would have asked, in light of the total honesty policy she'd installed between them. But he couldn't risk being off track again, couldn't risk another flat rejection. Most of all, he couldn't risk an honest answer he wasn't ready for.

Struggling not to storm after her, he let her walk away.

Viv walked away, all her will focused on not giving in to the urge to run. Run until she got far enough away from Ghaleb.

But she knew she could run to the other end of the earth and never be far enough away.

Everything had been going wrong ever since she'd set foot here, all the plans she'd made changing each minute, with Ghaleb doing one shocking thing after another to send her reeling, paralyzing her thinking, until she felt she couldn't carry one rational thought to its conclusion.

Coming here, she hadn't thought for a second that Ghaleb would show any interest in her again, would make any personal contact. She'd thought she'd go to work, observe him from afar, gather information about him and his situation, make her decision, leave.

But he was everywhere she turned, in the air she breathed, invading her mind and senses, establishing his dominion over her thoughts and responses, far deeper and more fully than before.

Oh, God, why was he doing this to her?

Was this about her not falling at his feet like she'd once done? Was he determined to have her there no matter what it took?

He'd almost had her there that first night. His incursion had taken her by storm, had made her let down her barriers, lulled her into a magical state of ease and companionship, until she'd forgotten why she was here, felt the past and all its pain fading away. Then she'd dared to resist his offer and he'd bared his fangs, jogging her out of her trance. Thankfully.

But he'd done her another favor. He'd laid the past to rest, solidified her resolve, showed her what mattered, the future, reminded her she was here for Sam's father, not her old lover.

Not that he was her old lover. In the past week he'd exposed her to sides of him he'd never cared to show her before, showing her he was a hundred times the man she'd lost her mind over…

She gasped as she stepped outside and the midnight warmth hit her after the controlled coolness of the center's interior. She saw Abdur-Ruhman leaning on his limo, waiting for her. He straightened at once to open her door for her.

She wanted to rush to him, jump in the car, as if that would cut her off from Ghaleb's emanations, snatch her from his field of influence. She could barely put one foot in front of the other.

And her depletion had nothing to do with coping with the demands of the job. In fact, switching from public relations wiz to suave executive to top surgeon, all while being an arbiter, a teacher and an example under the scrutiny of every eye in the center, would have been a challenge and a joy. If she wasn't doing it all a breath away from Ghaleb. Ghaleb, whose hands and eyes and breath meshed with hers during surgery, whose every word and glance and action sent every extreme emotion rioting inside her, whose focus on her was total, burning, gratifying, devastating.

*Ghaleb, who wanted her back in his bed.*

There. She'd thought it, faced it, put it into words.

He wanted to pick up from where he'd left off.

Even when his betrothal to some political bride was around the corner.

That had been the first thing she'd heard on her first gossip session in the center. Every woman bemoaning that the kingdom's—and probably the world's—most eligible bachelor was off the market at last, destroying even the luxury of fantasizing about him.

But it was clear he didn't consider his marriage of state anything to deter him from pursuing her. Why should it? As a sheikh and crown prince, he probably thought it his right to have a mistress. Or mistresses. And he wanted her to be among them, had just finished making her a staggering offer. She just had to name her price.

It was as clear to her now what had resurrected his interest. Her coming here had intrigued him, her irreverent attitude had roused the hunter in him, then her insistent attempts to keep her distance had inflamed him further. Now he was hungry. And getting hungrier with every moment she kept herself out of reach.

He'd launched his attack that first night, but when she'd struggled up for air, he'd left her no breathing room. He'd remained a foot away, showing her what it meant to be in the presence of superior intellect and skill, sucking her into the unparalleled pleasure of working with someone who seemed to know her thoughts as they formed, going all out to make her remember all she'd lost and how much more she could have now.

She'd realized what he'd been doing even before she'd admitted it to herself, and the effort she kept exerting to deter his invasion of her thoughts and senses, his overpowering of her will, had almost wrecked her.

She wobbled as she entered her limo and collapsed onto her seat.

She looked up at Abdur-Ruhman who looked down at her in alarm, tried a smile that came out a grimace. "Rough night."

"You work too hard, *ya sayedati*. As hard as Maolai Ghaleb." His eyes were both solicitous and reverent. *"Rubbena yehfathko lemann yehtajkom."*

She gave a weak giggle. "That sounded like an incantation."

"It's a prayer. Thanking God for you both and imploring Him to keep you safe for those who need you."

She attempted another tremulous smile, moved by his sincerity. He smiled down at her, at ease with her now, if still treating her like some sort of elevated creature, before he closed her door. She threw her head back, closed her eyes.

She could use his prayer. Its wisdom, if she couldn't have its protection. In case Ghaleb's temptation got too much for her.

She had to keep herself safe for Sam.

He was the only one who really needed her.

After Viv had disappeared from sight, Ghaleb headed to his private rooms on the surgical floor.

He whipped his sweatshirt over his head as he strode toward the shower, caught a glimpse of himself in the mirror...and came to a grinding halt.

*Ya Ullah,* had that wild look been in his eyes for long?

If it had been, it was merciful everyone had had eyes only for Viv today, that she'd barely looked at him as they'd spoken.

He exhaled heavily, tried to empty his gaze.

What was happening to him? What was *she* doing to him?

She'd invaded his life for three months, seven interminable years ago, after which time he'd been convinced he'd never see her again. Then eight days after exploding back into his life, she'd turned him inside out.

He opened his eyes, looked straight into his soul. He saw only chaos. Saw what he'd lived since birth believing would be his only path, a course filled with purpose and productivity, looking like a barren desert, a dark, empty, endless tunnel.

Was this crisis about her? Or was she just the catalyst?

So he wanted her, and she was a delight in every way. So he'd almost forgotten the past. So what? His situation remained unchanged, or it had changed for the worse. While she'd proved she wasn't here to forge a continuation of their affair, couldn't wait to go back to her own life. He should be thankful for that.

He wasn't. He had to have her again. This time he'd go in with his eyes open, taking what he wanted, giving her more than she could ever want. He couldn't resume his life otherwise.

And starting tomorrow he would launch his campaign to capture her. He wasn't stopping until she was his again.

Next morning he was in front of her door, assailed by the uncertainty he'd only ever felt on her account.

What if he couldn't reestablish their rapport? What if she insisted on shutting him out? He didn't want to resort to physical seduction, but he didn't know how much longer he could hold out…

*Enough. Get this done.*

Muttering an oath, he rang the bell.

Seconds later he heard running feet stampeding to the door.

Before he could process the fact that they sounded too fast, too light to be hers, the door rattled. Before surprise registered, the door was snatched open.

And he found himself looking down at a little boy.

A little boy who looked exactly like Viv.

# CHAPTER SIX

GHALEB FROZE, body and mind.

He could do nothing but stare at the boy.

The boy stared back at him.

It was the boy who shattered the trance, looking up at him in awe as he said, "Who are you?"

Who are *you?* Ghaleb wanted to groan back.

"Sam!"

The call splintered what remained of Ghaleb's daze, brought his eyes snapping up to the woman running down the stairs toward them. Not Viv. An older version of her. Someone related to her. Someone related to the boy. Someone too old to be his mother.

*What did that mean?*

He watched the woman approach, thunder crashing in his head.

"Prince Ghaleb?" the woman asked, her eyes, which were only a shade darker than Viv's, bright with certainty even when her question played it safe. He could only nod and her smile broke out, lively and tranquil at once as she extended a hand to him. "It's a pleasure to make your acquaintance, Your Highness. My name is Anna Cummings. I'm Vivienne's maternal aunt."

The boy tugged at his sleeve, snapping his eyes back to him. "I'm Sam. I'm six. Are you really a prince? Do you have a palace? And a horse? And a sword?"

"Sam!" Anna said reprovingly. "What do we do when we have guests?"

Sam looked crestfallen. "We don't ask them questions."

"And we don't keep them standing at the door." Anna turned apologetic, amused eyes to him. "Please, come in."

He took her hand automatically, let her lead him over the threshold Viv had denied him crossing. His eyes went back to the boy as if compelled, realizing why she had.

She hadn't wanted him to find out about the boy. Sam. Who was six. Sam, who was too young to be Anna's.

*Sam, who must be Viv's.*

Feeling like he was sinking in quicksand, he dropped down on the divan Anna had led him to in the spacious reception area, feeling betrayed all over again.

Judging by Sam's age, Viv must have had another relationship as soon as he'd left. She'd gone from his bed to someone else's without missing a beat. Or was it possible Sam was…?

Anna's good-natured voice interrupted his hurtling thoughts. "I want to thank you for all the amazing things you provided for us, Prince Ghaleb…"

He raised his hand, reference to his status now abrading his exposed nerves. "Just Ghaleb. And don't thank me, please. This is no more than what my honored guests deserve."

"You may not want to hear thanks…" she hesitated before letting that smile break out that was so like Viv's it was painful to behold "…Ghaleb, but I need to express them, so bear with me, okay?"

In spite of himself, he found himself smiling back at her. He didn't know whether it was her resemblance to Viv, her own soothing spirit or a mix of both, but he liked the woman. More, he connected with her. It was such a relief to have someone who offered him no more than the regard a host-cum-guest warranted, being clearly unaffected by his status.

"What do you mean, don't thank you?" Sam piped in. "Mom and Anna are always telling me to say thank you."

Even though it lacerated him to look at Sam, Ghaleb turned his eyes to him. "You don't enjoy saying thank you?"

"I don't understand why I should say it most of the time."

Ghaleb's lips twitched at Sam's earnest indignation, noticing that, while his behavior matched his age, his size belied it, being that of a boy two or more years older. His father must have been a big man. Someone as big as him. *Ya Ullah,* could it be…?

Anna interrupted his seething doubts again. "Now, Sam, how many times have we gone over this? You always say thank you when someone does or says something nice."

"I still don't understand why I should say thank you when Mrs. Callaway gives me stars. It's not nice. I earned them."

To his immense surprise Ghaleb laughed. It seemed Sam shared that power over him with his mother.

But he really understood and sympathized with Sam's reluctance. As a child, he'd had the same difficulty with thanking people for doing what they should do. He still had it when they didn't do a superlative job of it.

In all fairness, he was in such a position now he had to demand and expect everyone's best. It had still been imperative that he learned some humility, difficult as that had been, and to appreciate others' efforts. God rest his mother's soul.

He turned to Sam. "Mrs. Callaway earned your thanks, too, by being good at her job, by teaching you so well. That you made an effort doesn't make hers any less. But you don't have to say thank you if you don't want to. Just be the best student you can be, always be polite and hardworking and helpful. And on time."

Sam put his hand to his jaw, like an old professor deep in thought. "You mean that's saying thanks without saying thanks?"

Bright child. "Yes. But hearing the words can mean so much to her, can make her happy. Many times we say thank you just to make people feel good."

"Even if they didn't do anything really nice?"

"Does it have to be a big nice thing? Can't it be something small? Something they didn't have to do and still did it? And if they hear thanks they'll do it again, maybe bigger and better next time? But if they don't, they won't do it again, maybe even do nasty things instead?"

Sam's eyes went round, as if he'd made a huge discovery. "You mean saying thanks makes people want to be nice? Then keep on being nice?"

An extremely bright child. His smile broadened, even through the chaos that kept rising inside him. "Yes."

Sam turned to Anna. "Why didn't you and Mom just say so?"

Anna looked lost for words, before she let out a peal of laughter. "Oh, Ghaleb, see what you've done? His first man-to-man talk and us womenfolk are already guilty of misinforming him!"

Ghaleb started. His *first* man-to-man talk?

His father didn't maintain a relationship with him? Did he consider him a mistake, Viv's, and wanted no part of him? Or did Viv herself refuse him access to Sam now their relationship had ended? What *had* been the nature of that relationship? Could it be she didn't know whose son he was?

Could it be possible he was his…?

Sam tugged at him again. "Do you want to see my drawings?"

And even through the upheaval of insupportable doubts, Ghaleb smiled at Sam's crackling energy, so much like the old Viv's, the thing that had ensnared him on sight. "Yes. But I'll be honest in my opinion. Do you still want to show them to me?"

Sam gave that a moment's consideration, before he said importantly, "Only if you can draw good and show me how to do it."

"I can draw *well*. Very well, in fact. I am at my best drawing horses and falcons. I can show you how to draw those."

Sam gave a delighted yelp and zoomed out of the hall and stormed up the stairs.

As soon as he was out of view, Anna turned to Ghaleb. "Whew, that was weird. He doesn't take to strangers at all usually. In fact, he's been called difficult and unapproachable, and this whole thing about saying thank you and his teacher—well, it's part of what everyone has been calling his anti-social behavior."

Ghaleb was stunned. "I've never encountered a boy more eager to interact and capable of doing it than Sam."

"That's what I find so unusual. It must be you. You put him at ease when you should have intimidated him. Whatever it is, I'm grateful for it. Yes, it's another thing I'll thank you for, so you better grit your teeth and accept it."

He shook his head, the questions revolving inside it almost splitting it. They all fought to come out at once.

But when he could speak at last, a statement beat everything else to his lips. "You love him very much."

Anna's face became the embodiment of the emotion. "He's half my life. The other half is Vivienne. They are the grandson and the daughter I never had. Vivienne has always been like my daughter anyway, but she became even more so after my sister died."

Ghaleb felt as if he'd swallowed a handful of broken glass.

This was only underlining how right Viv had been. That he knew nothing about her. He'd never asked her about her life. And even when he'd realized the man he'd dealt with during exchanging funding for the hospital's research machine was her father, he hadn't made the least effort to get to know him. He'd actually made sure the man never contacted him in person again.

Had he not wanted to delve into her family life

because he hadn't cared, as she'd accused? Or because he'd known it would end and he hadn't wanted to get more involved with her? Whatever his motivation had been, everything amounted to the same result.

But he wanted to know everything now. He had to.

"You said this was Sam's first man-to-man talk," he said, struggling to leash the harshness of urgency, of resurrected anger and pain. "What happened to his father?"

Anna gave a resigned shrug. "I know nothing about him beyond that it was a fleeting liaison when Viv was at her lowest ebb. She never mentions him."

Ghaleb digested that like he would a handful of burning coal.

According to Sam's age, it must have happened as soon as he'd left. Had that been why she'd been at her lowest ebb? Had he meant something to her after all, and the way he'd treated her, the way he'd left her, had made her desperately seek solace?

The possibilities got too much for him. He escaped them, asked another question. "What about Viv's father?"

Anna looked taken aback before understanding dawned in her eyes. "Ah, you once worked in the same place as Robert and Vivienne. That's how you know him. You must have called her Viv then, too." That only solidified his suspicion that Viv hadn't told Anna about them. "And nothing happened to Robert. Last we heard he was honeymooning with his fifth bride. A woman ten years Vivienne's junior."

"Viv's parents were long divorced when I met her?"

Anna gave a sarcastic huff. "Since you met her some time after she'd been born, sure. The marriage lasted under a year. He'd married Laura for an inheritance that never materialized and walked out the moment she told him she was pregnant. He told her to abort the baby and was enraged when she didn't. He retaliated by never acknowledging Vivienne."

His stomach convulsed. "But she was working at the hospital where he was the director when we met."

"She'd been trying to see for herself if what we told her about Robert was the truth. She only learned we've been kind."

"He still rejected her?" he rasped.

"He did worse than that. He fired her, got her into an investigation for malpractice, almost got her license revoked. It was a harrowing fight to clear her name and nothing short of a miracle that she found another post."

This was it. The setback she'd mentioned. When her performance had suffered, and the people who'd wanted her out of their hair—her own father as it had turned out—had used it to get rid of her.

His jaw hurt, as did his hands with suppressing the vio-lence that erupted inside him, the need to go and take that man apart, *then* hit him where it would really hurt, cripple.

But had that been the time of her lowest ebb? She'd surrendered to the oblivion of a random liaison after she'd been let down by both her lover and father?

He could barely think or breathe, each word re-painting Viv's past from a pampered, privileged daughter to a discarded, abused one like a fresh skewer impaling him.

He *would* make that man suffer.

But he'd give Robert LaSalle his just deserts later. He didn't deserve attention now. Not when there were critical facts he needed to know, vital losses that had shaped Viv's life.

With the utmost difficulty, he brought his rage and aggression under control and grated, "When did your sister die?"

Sudden tears glittered in Anna's eyes as remembered pain swept her slightly withered beauty. "Four and a half years ago. From cervical cancer. But during the last stages, my husband, from whom I was separated, had a massive stroke and I had to go back to him. Vivienne supported us through it all, financially and medically. Then Laura and Joe died and I moved in with Vivienne and Sam."

Silence crashed in the wake of her word, leaving Ghaleb reeling under the blows of the revelations and realizations.

Viv had been in dire need of help so many times all these years. Yet she hadn't even tried to contact him to ask for anything. Had she believed he'd deny her support, as she'd accused him of denying her the most basic acknowledgment— the courtesy of a goodbye? Had she expected him to be as cruel and vindictive as that worthless bastard of a father had been? Worse still, having believed what he had about her, wouldn't he have been?

Worst of all, how could the woman he'd believed

had seduced him for what she could get out of him not even ask for any kind of help when she'd been in dire trouble? Trouble he could have easily found out the truth about, to determine the legitimacy of her appeals, that she wasn't trying to milk him by using another method—sympathy—when seduction had failed?

That could mean only one thing. He'd been totally wrong.

But if she hadn't wanted what all women wanted from him, money and luxury, why had she pursued him? When she'd answered her colleague's questions about him in that blithe tone, saying that he meant nothing to her? Had it been much simpler than he'd thought? Had it been only sex to her? But if it had been, why had she said she'd loved him? He could have understood this inexplicable fickleness had she been a teenager, not an adult and a doctor, the responsible one he'd discovered she'd always been.

Was this how men went insane, going around in circles of confusion and doubt?

But whatever her reasons had been, she hadn't only survived without his help, without anyone's help, when she'd been a new and single mother, she'd supported two families through one nightmare after another and come out stronger, more accomplished and more in control than he could have dreamed possible.

*Ya Ullah,* just how badly had he really misjudged her? Would it also turn out he'd hurt her as much, too?

"But that's all in the past now." Anna's words came as if in answer to his fraught questions, her overbright tone jarring him, even when he understood it was her effort to dispel the melancholy of reliving bad times. "Laura's at peace and Vivienne is getting what she deserves professionally and I have the privilege and pleasure of being with her and Sam."

"You're repaying Viv for her support by looking after Sam while she works?" he rasped.

She looked taken aback again before her face relaxed, once more serene and certain. "I can never repay her for all she's done, all she keeps doing for us. But it isn't like that between us. There are no debts or obligations. Vivienne is selfless to a fault, while I'm only blessed to have her and Sam."

After that declaration, he could only stare at her, his heart and mind flooding with too much chaos to navigate.

"I got all my colors!"

Ghaleb jerked around, infinitely grateful for the distraction of Sam's explosive return, as heart-wrenching as the sight of him, the very idea of him, was. A distressed guffaw burst from his depths as the boy hurled himself at him and dropped his armful of sketchbooks and drawing materials in his lap.

Crashing to a kneeling position at his feet, Sam anchored both hands on his knees and looked up at him with barely contained eagerness. "Tell me your opinion and teach me to draw a falcon."

Looking down at the cherubic face that had so much of Viv in it, overflowing with life and inquisitiveness and determination, Ghaleb felt upheaval dissipating and a different avalanche of emotions raging through him.

His voice was thick with their pressure as he said, "Why don't you show me your best work?"

Sam pounced on him, rummaged through the mess on his lap then pulled out one sketchbook and thrust it at him. "This."

With trembling hands Ghaleb leafed through the pages, his heart squeezing as he perused each effort, remarkable for a boy of his age, testimony to great talent…and turmoil. Was all this the manifestation of him being fatherless? A boy of such energy and intelligence, entering an age when he needed a strong and stabilizing male influence, his psyche suffering no matter how loving the females in his life were?

He pretended to examine each drawing at length, trying to bring his own turmoil under control.

At last he murmured, "You have what it takes to become a great artist. If you put your mind to it."

"You mean I'm good?" Sam whooped.

"Yes. But being good doesn't mean much without hard work."

"I work hard." Sam tugged at Anna. "Don't I?"

She nodded. "When you love something, you work very hard."

"That's good," Ghaleb said. "But you must always do your best, whether you love what you're doing or not. When you don't love something, you'll still be proud of your achievement and you'll make the world a better place. You may even end up loving it. When you're lucky to love something from the start, you just enjoy it more and your best might make you the best at it."

Sam hung on his every word as if he was memorizing them before he nodded his head vigorously.

Something burned behind Ghaleb's sternum

as he turned to a blank page. "We'll only need a pencil, a sharpener and an eraser."

Ghaleb's head spun at the speed with which Sam complied. In seconds he was blinking at the pencil that had been shoved in his hand as Anna chuckled and Sam bounced on the divan beside him, bubbling over with readiness for his first falcon-drawing lesson.

Gripping the pencil hard to control his tremors, Ghaleb started to sketch the general shape of the profile of a falcon, his favorite pose.

Sam hung on his every stroke as Ghaleb explained his actions. Before long he exclaimed, "Wow, you just drew a few lines and it already looks like a falcon!"

Ghaleb made the mistake of looking at Sam then and felt his lungs shut down. Sam's eyes were shining with budding hero-worship. And instead of being dismayed by it, he wanted to go all out to boost that expression, to deserve the adulation.

*Ya Ullah,* he shouldn't feel this toward Viv's son, the son whose father was unknown, who surely couldn't be him. Surely she would have told him if she'd even suspected it? He couldn't identify what "this" was, but it was too powerful, too...

"What are you doing here?"

His heart stopped. Breathless, his head jerked up and around.

And there she was. Viv. In another camouflaging outfit, fresh out of a shower or a bath, hair darkened with wetness, flushed, fragrant even at this distance. And as mad as hell that he was there.

How he *hungered* for her. And now that he knew how much she'd suffered, how much she'd endured, what she'd triumphed over, how much he'd mistreated her, the hunger gnawed at him, body and soul. And then there was Sam…

"That was a record-breaking bath." That was Anna, getting up, sounding cheery but throwing Viv a puzzled, admonishing look. "I was about to come and see what had taken you so long."

Viv had eyes only for Ghaleb. Stormy eyes. She was as angry with him now as she had been that first night. Angrier.

The turbulence lasted seconds before she wrestled it under control for the others' benefit. With a tight smile she turned her gaze to Anna and Sam.

"Okay, guys," she said, her voice brittle with forced lightness. "How about you get ready to go out to explore Jobail? I'll talk business with Prince Ghaleb before heading to work."

"But, *Mo-om!* Ghaleb is showing me how to draw a falcon."

Viv couldn't have looked more shocked if Sam had told her he was showing him how to *become* one. Following shock came something like horror. Then fury was back, more forceful than before.

She still brought it under control, avoiding his gaze as she addressed her son. "Sam, you don't call older people by their first names—"

Sam interrupted her. "I call Anna by her first name."

"That's different, darling."

"Different how? And he *said* to call him Ghaleb. And he is teaching me to draw falcons and horses." He snatched the sketchbook off Ghaleb's lap. "Look."

Viv looked, her color draining before she visibly struggled to pin a smile on her strained face. "That's nice, darling, but…*Ghaleb* isn't here to teach you to draw. He's here to talk about work with me and he's a very busy man. So, please, go up with Anna to get ready. And say thank you to Ghaleb for being so nice."

At that Sam looked at him and they both burst out laughing.

Viv gasped, her eyes stricken as they slammed from him to Sam. They ended up drilling him with another glare before she turned to Sam again. "I'd love to be in on the joke but I have important things to discuss with Ghaleb now, then I must rush to work. Later?"

Sam's face fell as he started mumbling, succumbing to his mother's insistence and gathering his things.

"Gentlemen don't mumble, Sam," Ghaleb admonished, firm yet gentle. Sam shot him a beleaguered look. "They don't sulk either."

At that Sam tried to clear his face, looking adorably stoic in his efforts. If anything, Ghaleb felt that increasing Viv's irritation and impatience.

Suddenly Sam threw himself at him and gave him a fierce hug.

A hush fell. It was as if every heart had stopped until Sam reluctantly unclasped his arms from Ghaleb's neck and scrambled off the divan to join a clearly moved Anna.

Suffering a nervous disruption from Sam's impulsive hug, he met Viv's turbulent eyes.

She didn't want him there. She didn't want him near her family. Near Sam. That was painfully clear. If it was up to her, he'd never lay eyes on either Anna or Sam again. Especially Sam.

It shouldn't bother him. He should even think it the prudent thing to do. The sane thing to do. Not to get involved.

But he cared nothing about prudence and sanity anymore. He felt already involved. He was, with her. And he had to see more of Sam. He had to see more of Viv as a protective mother, another unsuspected side to her. He would.

He rose to his feet as Anna and Sam walked to the stairs. "One of my best drivers, Jameel, is waiting outside to take you wherever you want to go. He speaks perfect English and knows Jobail inside out and will make you the best guide possible."

"But we can't take your driver!" Anna exclaimed.

"My driver is Abdur-Ruhman." He turned his eyes on Viv at her gasp of surprise. "I couldn't entrust anyone but him to give you the best service, but now you've been so kind that you wouldn't let him stay here, you did us all a favor, not only him. He lives at my palace, which is far from the center, and that's why I thought it best for him to stay here rather than commute. Now he'll be with me as usual and we'll pick you up each morning. On the return journey we'll drop you off first."

He held her sullen gaze as she digested his new decision then added, "And contrary to being here to talk about work, I'm only here to escort you to work. And I'm so glad I came and made the acquaintance of your delightful family." He turned to Anna and Sam. "And now that I have, I hope you'll all agree to honor me by accepting my invitation to dinner tomorrow night."

Viv stared out at Jobail rushing by, feeling numb.

It was all spiraling out of control.

He'd seen Sam.

She pressed her fist to her chest, her heart almost coming to a standstill as it had when she'd come down to find Ghaleb sitting with Anna and Sam, the three of them absorbed in each other, at ease, an image of domestic bliss.

She'd panicked, had turned almost vicious.

Oh, God, she shouldn't have brought them here!

But she couldn't have left them. She'd never

left Sam for more than the hours she'd spent at work. Two months away from him, leaving him and Anna alone, let alone that long, hadn't been something she'd even contemplated.

But in her original plan, the one that seemed totally moronic now, Ghaleb wasn't supposed to ever see them. There shouldn't have been any reason or situation where he would.

But he had, and she was totally unprepared for this turn of events. To make it worse still, in the minutes she'd had with Anna before she'd marched out ahead of Ghaleb to the limo, Anna had confessed she'd "talked" to Ghaleb. Translation: she'd told him everything. Everything she knew. The one secret to survive disclosure had been the one she didn't know.

The identity of Sam's father...

*He'd been teaching Sam how to draw falcons.*

Memories assailed her again, like a rapid photo montage. Ghaleb sitting between Anna and Sam, large and majestic, commanding their awe. Sam gazing at him as if he recognized him, seeking physical contact in restless touches, like a cat stroking agitatedly against its owner after a long absence. Sam throwing his arms around Ghaleb and hanging on as if to a lifeline. Ghaleb's face, filled with shock and agitation and…tenderness?

The memories were as heart-crushing as they'd been in reality. Oh, God… She flopped her head against the door as waves of nausea overcame her.

She hadn't dreamed of this scenario. That Anna and Sam would see Ghaleb and be as entranced as she'd once been. While he…

Was he as interested in them as he'd seemed? Or was he only using them to get to her? He knew she wouldn't have agreed to another invitation. But with Sam and Anna beside themselves with excitement to accept, he'd gained her agreement.

"Don't you think you've fumed in silence long enough?"

Every muscle in her body clenched at having his dark, rich voice pouring over her every inflamed nerve ending.

He had *way* too much of everything. And he was using it all on her. Why? All that because she'd intrigued him, resisted him? His ego was that big?

*Well, moron, he's a sheikh, a crown prince, a world-class surgeon and the world's most magnificent male. What do you think?*

Without looking at him, she said, "Have you started the search for a new co-head, Ghaleb? You have less than seven weeks before I go, and you may want to have someone sooner than that so I can save you the trouble of breaking them in as you've been doing with me."

"Stop it, Viv." That had been a growl, one to put the predator she'd likened him to to shame. "I'm not searching for a replacement. In fact, I told Adnan to do so the moment I saw you, but I told him to stop the search the very next day."

"You shouldn't have done that. I am leaving when my contract is up."

"I don't understand why you're persisting with this. You have your family with you, the job you have here is light years beyond anything you can have in your country, and Anna told me—"

"Our life story, evidently. And as evidently you feel sorry for us. Well, don't. We're fine."

His hand burned her flesh as he turned her face to him. His was ablaze with aggravation. "I can *see* you're fine, and I'm not sorry for you. I'm sorry for what I believed, the way I behaved. I did have extenuating reasons but—"

She cut him off again, her voice low. "But I'm

not interested in discussing them and neither am I here to make peace with you."

His eyes clashed with hers, demanding that she retreat, give in. She held her ground.

His jaw tensing, he muttered, "You didn't tell me you had a son."

God, no. She wasn't ready for this. Please, please…

She resorted to her only defense when she was cornered— turned sarcastic. "You didn't ask."

"I'm asking now. Who is his father?"

"What is it to you?"

"He's six. I need to know if he is—"

"He's mine. His father is someone I barely knew. Someone who disappeared from my life before I found out I was pregnant."

"You didn't give him the choice of being a part of his son's life?"

"No. It wasn't a relationship and the last thing he could have wanted was a son, messing up his life and plans. My pregnancy was a mistake on my side, but that wasn't the father's business. But though Sam wasn't planned, I never for a moment regretted the way things have worked out. I wanted Sam with everything in me. He's everything I live for."

The suspicion in his eyes died. And what was that dulling of the intensity? Relief? Disappointment? Neither?

The evasions, the lies, chafed her insides until she felt she couldn't breathe.

But she couldn't tell him. Not like this. She didn't want to be forced into telling him. Not when she didn't know if she even should, how he would react, if it would come to anything, change anything between them…

"Sam could have been ours…under different circumstances." Ghaleb's voice was a bass rasp, so deep, so hushed it was almost unintelligible, as if he were talking to himself.

"I'm sure that would have been such a delight to you. The woman you warned from day one that she was a passing fling coming to you with news of your impending fatherhood. Just imagine yourself, duty-bound and having something like that thrown at you. Would you have chosen me over duty if you'd known I was carrying your child? No, you wouldn't."

"You're probably right."

She'd known that. But hearing him say it validated her decision to keep Sam her secret, but flooded her with misery at the same time.

He was silent until she thought he wouldn't talk again. Then he finally exhaled. "And, Viv…tomorrow night is still on."

# CHAPTER SEVEN

VIV TRIED ONE LAST time to make her fingers obey her mental commands. They didn't and she gave up, dropped her hands, let the hairpin clatter to the dresser.

She stared at herself in the mirror, winced at the failed attempt at a chignon. At the scared look in her eyes.

Ghaleb would be arriving any moment now.

He'd said seven sharp. He sure loved that number. He'd called her at seven in the morning to tell her not to bother getting out of bed. He'd decreed she'd take the day off. She hadn't argued.

The past week had to go down as her life's most depleting. Or she was just losing her stamina. Or had already lost it.

Yesterday, going to work and getting embroiled into another brutally testing day, after the upheaval of Ghaleb's visit and its repercussions had been harrowing. It had been a miracle that she'd held up, hadn't collapsed into a gibbering mess by the end of the list.

She caught sight of her trembling lips, looked down at her shaking hands and gave a sarcastic laugh. Sure, she'd held up. Look at how she was holding up now. The epitome of stability…

"Mo-om, Ghaleb's here!"

She lurched, swayed, almost collapsed where she stood.

He was here. *Here.* Right on time for another round. And this time he had allies in his campaign against her. Her own family. The excitement in Sam's call, his elation at Ghaleb's arrival, had been unmistakable.

Suddenly she wanted to put an end to all the uncertainty and turmoil. Just go down and tell them all the truth.

She couldn't. She no longer even knew if it was possible to tell Ghaleb the truth, let him decide what to do with it. She'd been reading up on current events in Omraania and watching the local news every chance she'd got since she'd arrived. She'd learned how truly different things were here, what being the crown prince of Omraania meant. Worst of all, Ghaleb's future state marriage had the objective of producing an heir to cement vital relationships with one of their neighboring kingdoms. It would probably be catastrophic for him and the monarchy for an illegitimate son of his to be discovered now.

She had to have more time to consider the ramifications, come up with a decision that wouldn't end up creating a far bigger problem than the one she alone was mired in now.

*"Mo-om!"*

Sam's impatient yell convinced her that whatever time she needed, it wasn't now. She snatched out the hairpins holding her hair up, shook it down, gave her disheveled reflection a pained grimace. That was followed by a mental smack for wanting to look sophisticated, for caring about her appearance at all in Ghaleb's eyes.

She grabbed her purse and ran out of the room. She slowed down the moment she came out to the hall leading to the stairs. She couldn't have Ghaleb thinking she was running so she wouldn't keep him waiting.

It was a good thing she'd slowed down, otherwise she might have collapsed down the whole flight of stairs. The sight that greeted her at the bottom was something that made her heart stumble and her legs almost give out.

Ghaleb was standing there with Sam and Anna. In full royal garb. His head was covered in the traditional white *ghotrah* held in place by the black *eggal,* a black, gold-trimmed *abaya* draping his formidable shoulders and cascading over a pristine white *taub* crisscrossed by heavy, black leather belts buckled at their meeting point, ending in one spanning his waist, with a chunky gold buckle where a ceremonial curved dagger sheathed in a worked silver scabbard hung.

And if she'd thought he'd looked indescribable in a suit the other night, she was at a loss for words now.

He stood there, looking up at her as she somehow kept coming down, his eyes engulfing her whole, as his hand engulfed Sam's. Sam who looked about to burst with excitement. Sam who, standing by Ghaleb, even with the differences in coloring, looked so much like him, a part of him…

"Why didn't you tell me you were inviting us to a fancy-dress party?" It took her a second to realize it had been her who'd said that. Without volition, more spilled from her lips, sending the black flames in his eyes raging higher. "I would have brought along my Grim Reaper costume."

Anna suppressed an embarrassed chuckle. Ghaleb's eyes promised retribution. Later.

For now he only drawled, "I thought I'd give you a fuller glimpse into Omraania, dress the part. As for you in a Grim Reaper costume—what a waste that would be. You in an Arabian princess costume on the other hand—that's far more fitting."

*Really? Maybe you can get your future bride to donate one.*

The bitterness mercifully shrilled only inside her mind.

But that it did at all...!

God, he was messing her up, messing with her mind.

"Look, Mom, look." Sam dropped Ghaleb's hand to run around him before snatching it up again. "He's really a prince. This is a real royal dagger. And he's taking us to—to...*el barr!*"

*"El barr?"* she repeated hollowly, her eyes prisoner to Ghaleb's.

He took a slow step closer. "It's the opposite of *el bahr,* the sea, literally meaning land, which is what we call the desert, especially when we're heading into it to differentiate from going to the seaside."

He extended an inviting hand to her as he spoke, one she took without thought, only to have her mind screeching for her to snatch it away when his warm, powerful hand engulfed hers and she found him holding both her and Sam to him and, after nodding courteously to Anna to precede them, steering them outside. He tightened his hold as if sensing her impending withdrawal.

Feeling robbed of her will, she walked outside beside him, saw Abdur-Ruhman waiting by a limo, met his welcoming smile with a dazed one as he rushed to open the door for them. Sam bounded on ahead and hurled himself onto the seat behind the driver's. Anna followed. She ended up beside Ghaleb on the backseat. He'd somehow kept her hand in his.

They drove until they came to a stop in a huge open space. In seconds Abdur-Ruhman came around to open the doors for them. Sam bounced out of the car full of questions.

"Why did we stop? Why did we get out of the car? What are we doing here?"

Before the same questions registered in Viv's mind, she heard what sounded like approaching thunder.

She looked up in disbelief, and there they were, floodlights on, zooming toward them, two huge helicopters. As she gaped, they landed a few dozen feet away and she found herself dragged by Sam, who was beside himself with excitement, running in his wake toward them. She looked back at Ghaleb in agitation, found his steady gaze on her as he strode behind them, with Anna's hand tucked in the crook of his arm.

He raised his hand and the helicopters' rotors slowed down so that they didn't have to struggle against the dust being kicked up.

"Can I sit in front? Can I?" Sam turned to Ghaleb, squeaking the question as soon as the noise abated, giving Viv a mental image of a puppy wagging his tail so hard he seemed to be dancing.

Ghaleb looked at her. "If your mother agrees."

"Is it safe?" Viv croaked. "To fly at all? I hear about sandstorms coming out of nowhere…"

"There is no possibility of one, or I wouldn't have proposed going to *el barr* at all. And if Sam promises to stay strapped in, it's totally safe for him to sit beside the pilot."

Sam looked up at her, bubbling over with expectation until she nodded, then he streaked to jump inside the first chopper.

They followed him, while Abdur-Ruhman went to the other chopper full of men, no doubt Ghaleb's bodyguards, and in minutes they were lifting off into the air.

Viv felt her lungs empty as she watched the ground recede. As if feeling her rising apprehension, Ghaleb squeezed her hand. She squeezed back, thankful for his grip.

He leaned closer, enveloping her in his warmth as he urged, his voice full of concern, "Don't look down if it bothers you."

She let herself sink against him, unable to stop even when her mind flayed her for being such a baby, for turning to him for comfort. "It's—it's just the first time I've flown—in a helicopter, I mean. It's very different than flying in a jet…very immediate, very real, if you know what I mean."

His eyes gleamed down at her in the subdued lighting, belying his calm voice, turbulent, tempestuous, his breath steaming against her cheek, singeing her. "I know. You quickly get used to it."

And she knew that if Anna and Sam hadn't been sitting with them, he would have let loose the full measure of his hunger on her, crushed her to him, his hands seeking out her secrets and pleasures, his mouth dominating hers, finishing her.

She closed her eyes to quell the urge to surrender her sanity, to raise her face to his, to beg him not to hold back.

It took her moments to collect herself and push out of his loose hold, ignoring his seething frustration as she did her own.

For the rest of the flight she concentrated on following the moon as it hid then emerged from behind clouds, feeling all her blood gravitating toward him, pulling at her, her resistance tearing at her. She ignored the conversation Anna started with Ghaleb, one Sam kept interrupting at all the wrong times, putting in something totally off track and hilarious, having misheard what was being said over the noise of the engine, drawing Anna's laughter. Viv didn't laugh. She felt like weeping instead. Ghaleb at first sat beside her, his tension reverberating with hers, but he eventually let go, surrendered to his enjoyment of the others' interaction, teasing them until he had them in stitches. Every laugh was one more skewer turning in her heart.

As soon as they landed, his hand sought hers again. She snatched it away this time. His eyes hardened with aggravation for a moment, before challenge replaced it. He knew what she felt, knew how hard she was trying not to succumb. He was also certain she would.

She glared back. *Never again.*

"Don't be so sure," he muttered, his exotic accent, which had buried her under its intoxicating weight from the first syllable he'd uttered, stretching over her, sliding across her exposed nerves.

She gasped at the jolt of stimulation. At the import of his words. He'd heard her thoughts, was taking up the challenge.

He turned away, helping Anna out of the chopper, leaving *her* to disembark on her own.

The moment she'd done so, she again felt as if she'd set foot in the past, that of a culture she'd only ever heard about but had failed miserably to imagine.

The scene in front of her was totally alien, the ambiance overpowering in its richness and depth and purity.

Nestled against a craggy mountain that rose in the middle of an ocean of sand dunes, an ancient wall soared up, shielding the battlements of a breathtaking castle. It loomed against the sky, only the strewn campfires of a nomadic Bedouin encampment huddling in its protection shedding fluctuating light on it.

Sam ran on ahead then ran back, only to run ahead again, urging them to go faster. Anna, clearly as enchanted, strode ahead to accommodate his enthusiasm. Ghaleb's men had all disappeared, leaving only him in her vicinity. He waited for her but when she again ignored him, he kept his reaction silent and walked by her side until they'd caught up with Anna and Sam.

"What's this place? What's it called? Does it have a name? Do these people live here? In tents?"

She blinked at Sam's rapid-fire questions, at the sight of the camels roving free among the camel-hair tents.

Ghaleb smiled down at him. "All right, one question at a time. Yes, this place does have a name, and it's Az-Zaferah. That means the victor, only a female victor..."

"Victoria," Sam put in, very seriously.

One of Ghaleb's eyebrows shot up in surprise before his smile widened. "Of course, but you, clever boy, are absolutely right. *Zaferah is Victoria.* Wait until I tell my brothers what none of us had thought of all these years."

"You have brothers?" That seemed to excite Sam very much.

It only oppressed Viv. Ghaleb had never told her he had brothers. Had he ever told her anything relevant? But then again, why should he have told her anything? His temporary good-time woman? The role he wanted her to play again when he wanted to wind down between important pursuits?

He didn't notice her plunging mood as he had eyes only for Sam now. "I have three brothers and one sister."

"You must be very happy!" Sam exclaimed.

Ghaleb snorted. "Having siblings is a mixed blessing. They do make me happy sometimes, but nobody can make me as miserable as they can…" He stopped, as if he'd realized he'd uttered a lie, his gaze sliding to her, disturbed, disturbing.

Was he thinking *she* could make him more miserable than his siblings?

Just as she kicked herself for even entertaining the idea that she mattered, had any effect on him at all, let alone something of this gravity, his eyes went opaque. "So, having siblings has its ups and downs. Being the oldest doesn't help. It makes me worry about them all the time."

"Like Mom always worries about me?" Sam asked. "It makes her so upset sometimes."

Ghaleb's eyes slid to her again. "Yes, exactly like that."

Sam gave it one more second of thought then declared, "I'd still like to have brothers. Maybe one sister, too, like you."

Viv's heart punched her ribs. Oh, God. For this particular matter to raise its ugly head now, in Ghaleb's presence! What if Sam's main concern, his lack of a father, followed?

Before she could think of something to say to divert that catastrophe, Anna, bless her, did, deliberately, as a snatched glance at her confirmed.

"You were telling us about Az-Zaferah?" Anna said as she started walking again, making them all move on.

Ghaleb's answering smile was still tight as he said, "Az-Zaferah is the Aal Omraans' ancestral home. It was their stronghold until the late nineteenth century when King Numair, my father's great-grandfather, switched his headquarters to Jobail, leaving this place to gradually fall into decay."

He suddenly picked Sam up. Sam immediately made himself comfortable in his arms, wrapping his own around Ghaleb's neck, enjoying the higher vantage point and having Ghaleb's undivided attention. The sight of father and son together made Viv's heart thud.

If only…

Oblivious to her state, Ghaleb went on, explaining to Sam, "Decay means it was not maintained until it began to fall apart." He turned to her and Anna. "That was until I decided it was too precious and had it restored. Soon I hope it will become one of Omraania's most frequented historical sites, and tourists can wander through its maze of walls, houses and palaces."

"You mean it's not only a castle behind those walls?" That was Anna, sounding as fascinated as Sam.

Ghaleb shook his head. "It was a big fortified town once upon a time."

Sam jumped in his arms. "Can we be the first tourists?"

Ghaleb ruffled his hair. "That's why I brought you here. We'll spend the night, and in the morning we'll go exploring."

Viv's alarm soared. "Spend the night?"

Ghaleb gave her a mock-serene look. "It's called camping."

Failing to read Viv's reaction this time, and clearly as excited as Sam at the prospect of spending the night there, Anna asked, "Will we stay with the Bedouins?"

Ghaleb's smile was indulgent, encompassing Anna and Sam. "We'll spend part of the night with them. I think you'll enjoy seeing how they live. They're so glad to have you tonight, they'll give one of their feasts in your honor."

Viv gave him a sullen glance. "You mean in yours."

"In mine, too," he agreed easily. "It's not every day their crown prince comes visiting." He waited for the expected I-told-you-so to flare in her eyes before going on smoothly. "Not that I'm putting them out. Feasts are regular occasions for them. Every wedding, birth, coming of age and religious occasion is a feast. Singing and dancing and preparing banquets are regular occurrences so our presence is one more excuse for them to do what they enjoy doing most." His gaze left her chagrined eyes to seek those of his most willing admirers. "Afterwards, we'll spend the night in our camp, over there."

They all followed his pointing finger. Viv couldn't believe she hadn't noticed the camp before. But it must have either been shrouded in darkness or not erected yet. Now, in the dual illumination of the rising moon and a now raging fire, a much bigger and more sophisticated one than the Bedouins', two huge tents were flanked by six others at the top of the highest dune, their whiteness silvered by moonbeams and gilded by flickering flames.

"I bet you're getting hungry." Ghaleb started walking toward the encampment again. "I hope you like barbeques. That's mostly what *El Badu* will offer us tonight. Of course, if you don't like it, I'm ready for that contingency."

"Who doesn't like barbeques?" Anna laughed. "And I bet even if anyone doesn't, that smell alone can convert them."

Ghaleb had to be satisfied with that and Sam's enthusiastic agreement. Viv wasn't going to comment on her food preferences now. She felt almost sick to her stomach as it was.

"To answer your last questions, Sam, about the people here, yes, they do live in tents but, no, they don't live here. They're *Badu*—in English, Bedouins. They are nomads who move from one place to another in search of water for themselves and pasture for their animals. They've come here since I've restored the wells, but though I did offer to make their stay permanent, they insisted they couldn't stay in one place, had to move around."

"Even if they have water and past—paste—" Sam frowned in his effort to repeat the word.

"Pasture," Ghaleb supplied with a smile, pronouncing it slowly. "That's grazing grounds, land rich in grass for their animals to eat. Yes, it's what they are, people who don't settle in one place, and usually people can't change what they are."

Viv felt her heart shrivel at that statement. She knew he couldn't even see the relevance, how that pertained to him, but she did. Ghaleb was what he was, and that made him off-limits. To Sam. She had nothing to do with it.

Her thoughts ceased then vanished as dozens of men and women advanced on them, loud, enthusiastic, welcoming them before they rushed ahead again, hurrying them to their destination.

"What is that boy wearing on his head?" Sam pointed toward one of the boys who was closest to them, looking at Ghaleb in utter awe. "It isn't like your—your…"

"My white headdress is called *ghotrah*. His red and white patterned one is called *shmagh*."

"I like his better. It's cool. Can I wear one?"

"You certainly can." Ghaleb motioned to a man who seemed to be the tribe's sheikh and arranged for Sam to have a *shmagh*.

In a minute Ghaleb lowered Sam to the ground and he ran to the boy who shook his hand importantly then started to show off his *shmagh*-wrapping skills.

"This is the most exciting thing that has ever happened to me," Anna declared, her voice and eyes sparkling with pleasure.

Ghaleb responded with a satisfied smile as he gave her his arm, leaving Viv to stumble in their wake.

Viv somehow ended up sitting beside him on the handwoven carpets on the sand as the *Badu* served them date wine, *kapsa* rice and a stunning assortment of barbequed meats. According to Anna and Sam, everything was "divine" and "yummy" respectively. She wouldn't know. With Ghaleb bombarding her with his heat and hunger, anything she put in her mouth tasted like ashes.

She was about to excuse herself and walk back to their camp when an eruption of thuds made her jump.

Ghaleb's arms were instantly around her,

soothing. "The matrons of the tribe are just heralding the entertainment."

Her eyes went to the source of the pounding—older women in black, with their faces uncovered and tattooed. One of them was two feet behind her.

"They do so by pounding…" She squinted at the foot-tall container the woman was whacking away at with a two-foot pestle. "What *are* they pounding?"

He smiled into her eyes. "That's a *mihbaj,* a wooden grinder, which they use to grind their coffee, sometimes other seeds, but it also constitutes one of their main percussion instruments."

As he spoke, a storm of percussion rose. "Ah, now the rest have joined in." He pointed out each instrument, shouting now over the clamor. "The small tambourine is called *reg,* the big one without the jangles is *duff,* and those guys keeping that hot rhythm are playing on the *darabukkah,* that vase-shaped hand drum. After that rousing introduction, melody players will join in."

Sure enough, a melodic droning started, emanating from some sort of stringed instrument, a skin-covered box, along with the squealing and whining of reedlike wind instruments, drowning his voice completely.

He put his lips to her ear to be heard, jolting more bolts of stimulation through her. "That's the *rababah,* their main melody instrument. And, yes, all that sound *is* produced from a single string of horsehair and a bow. Those enthusiastic lads are playing the high-pitched, double-reed *mizmar,* with the sedate and experienced musicians playing the more evocative single-reed *naay.*"

"You sure know your cultural music," she gasped, drowning, in him, in the hyper-reality of it all.

"Knowing the names of the instruments hardly makes me an expert. But, yes, I know how to play an instrument or two, if you'd care for a demonstration later. In private."

She pulled away from him as if he'd scalded her. He gave her a long, considering glance, no doubt weighing his reaction. He ended up bunching his jaw muscles, deciding not to press her, for either response or resumed closeness.

She sat there staring ahead, trying to shut him out of her focus. It should have been possible with that mesmerizing spectacle unfolding before her eyes. And, dammit, this was probably a once-in-a-lifetime experience. She *should* be enjoying it.

As if sensing everything passing through her mind, he leaned closer, whispered in her ear, "Just let go, Viv. Enjoy this now."

She snatched a look into his eyes, every hurt she'd ever suffered rushing to hers. She felt rather than heard him groan. Then, with a gentle touch, he turned her face away and toward the display.

Still trembling, she forced herself to watch as the young men of the tribe, in their layered and flowing robes and *shmaghs,* came forward with gleaming swords. A row of women followed to form a line facing them, wearing black dresses and head coverings embroidered in cross-stitch designs.

"The head covering designs are blue for unmarried women, red for married," Ghaleb shouted over the music, inviting her to clap to the rhythm. She reluctantly started to, noticing that Anna had been swept in the unbridled energy of the performance, while Sam was rushing with the boy he'd befriended to the middle of the dance arena, imitating the dance steps uninhibitedly.

Suddenly Viv found herself being encroached

on by the dancing women, as the men did on Ghaleb, being pulled to her feet and thrust into the middle of a dancing circle with him as the singers and dancers escalated their enthusiasm.

"You put them up to this!" she accused.

She knew he could only read her lips, but that he did it perfectly. In answer he smiled broadly down at her, giving her no clue if he had master-minded this or not, prodding her to move along with him to a simple dance step.

Or she thought it simple until she tried it and her feet stumbled over each other. Ghaleb raised a hand at once and the beat immediately slowed down to a manageable pace, until she started moving with him to the primal beat, to the haunting, raw music, her heart keeping tempo.

And she found herself transported into another realm where nothing existed but him. She felt him, and only him, as his eyes dominated her, lured her, soothed her, inflamed her, as he moved *with* her as if he was connected to her on the most fundamental levels, moved *her* as if it was his will that powered her body, his mind that ruled her thoughts.

They went on for hours, dancing, resting, dancing again. She even tried singing one of their songs, to the roaring approval of the crowd, the kind souls.

It could have been minutes or hours when the music came to an end. She couldn't tell the time anymore, felt she was wading in a dream state. She was only jogged out of it when Sam ran back to them, flushed and petulant.

"I want more dances and songs!" he cried.

She knew she should say something to him, yet couldn't.

It was Anna who said, "The *Badu* were so generous, Sam, gave us such a great evening that you should be thanking them, not asking for more."

"But it's still early. Why can't they sing and dance some more?"

"And if they do, do you think you'll have enough?" Ghaleb went down on his haunches before him. "We don't ever have enough of what we enjoy and love, Sam. But we can cherish what we have of it, and if it comes to an end, instead of feeling bad, we should be thankful we had it at all. Then we can always remember it and feel happy each time we do."

The outraged, frustrated Sam calmed down as if by magic and nodded. Viv's throat convulsed. Oh, God, the way Ghaleb reached him so effortlessly, the way Sam responded to him, with such trust.

She felt Ghaleb taking her arm, walking her to their hosts, where they gave their thanks. She was unsure if she talked or smiled or just stood there looking like a drugged idiot.

Ghaleb steered them from the encampment and up to their camp, again carrying Sam. Sam who was tired in spite of his earlier demand for more entertainment, Sam who melted into him. Sam who balked at any prolonged body contact and most forms of physical affection.

Viv put one foot in front of the other, her thoughts and emotions in meltdown, her eyes prisoner to the sight of father and son, both oblivious to their vital connection.

Suddenly Sam sighed. "There are a million stars up there."

She heard Ghaleb's smile in his voice. "There are way more than a million stars in the Milky Way, our galaxy, but though you'll never see clearer skies or brighter stars anywhere in the world, we can only see around eight thousand."

"Did you count them?" Sam asked, his voice more sleepy.

Ghaleb gave a self-deprecating chuckle. "I

tried. I always lost count. That number is what scientists say. But I don't need to know how many stars I can see to enjoy them."

Sam yawned. "Neither do I. I never saw many stars where we lived." Sam sounded bereft, then perked up again. "But now we live here I'll get to see them and even know their names. Will you find them out and teach them to me?"

"I'll teach you everything you want to learn."

Viv's heart seized. What was he *doing,* promising something like that? Making it sound like a solemn vow?

But he had. And it sounded as if he'd meant it, too.

What did that mean?

Whatever he'd meant, this could go one of two ways. Either Ghaleb was really interested in Sam, and she'd tell him the truth once they'd left and he'd maintain some kind of relationship with his son. Or his situation would force him not to, and she'd have to perform damage control, the damage that had already been done from the moment Sam had seen Ghaleb.

But as she watched him holding Sam as he fell asleep in his arms, everything told her he would do right by his son. He might not be able to acknowledge him, but he'd want to be in his life. They might work out something that would be best for Sam.

And that was why, no matter how he made her feel, she couldn't have anything with him again. Whatever they had would end badly again, would cast shadows over or even jeopardize any future relationship he and Sam might be able to have.

She'd seen enough since she'd been here to learn that he was a noble man, a great man. It was just that he'd never had a place in his life for someone like her. For anything beside duty. It had been her mistake. She'd hurled herself there, when he'd warned her not to.

So why was he pursuing her now? Did he think he could make sure an affair with her now wouldn't have any repercussions on his status? Did he think she was free to have another affair with him and feeling her equal desire and thinking as he did that the past belonged in the past, he didn't understand her resistance?

Not knowing what to feel, think or do, she was mute for the rest of the way, thankful that the others had fallen silent, too.

Ghaleb led them to the biggest tent, entered ahead to put Sam to bed in one of the compartments. Viv made sure Sam was sound asleep before she stumbled out and into the adjacent compartment.

The moment she was inside she turned, swaying, saw Ghaleb's silhouette pausing on the other side of the fabric wall. She struggled for air as she felt the urge rising inside him to sweep the barrier aside, to storm in and break down her resistance.

Anna's silhouette joined his as she murmured heartfelt thanks and good-night. Viv heard his voice vibrating before Anna moved on. Then he turned toward her again.

Just as she thought he would act on his urge, he finally moved away. She crumpled to the floor.

She lay listening to the howling of the wind, praying for exhaustion to claim her.

It didn't. Ghaleb's pursuit had chased away peace, control, paralyzed her, made her unable to be rational.

If only he'd stop, leave her alone…

It might have been hours before the shadows cast by the lantern illuminating her compartment started playing havoc with her imagination, turning the spacious area into a claustrophobic trap. She rose, tiptoed outside, desperate for air, for space.

It was even worse outside. No one could know how majestic and humbling, how downright terrifying and absolutely alien night could be until they'd been in the desert at night. The eerie silver oceans of sand and the shadows created by the dunes made her realize how Middle Eastern fables had come to such vivid and sometimes macabre life. She certainly felt a genie or worse would materialize at any time, and not to grant her three wishes.

"You couldn't sleep either."

*Ghaleb.* Of course. Genies had nothing on him. His men must be around, too, somewhere.

She remained frozen until he swathed her in a huge cashmere shawl that seemed to generate instant heat, making her realize she had been freezing. The change of temperature sent a shudder through her. He gathered her against his body, his arms tightening, his head dipping to hers, his breath steaming against her face, her neck. "Viv, stop pushing me away."

She did just that, struggled out of his arms.

He advanced on her again, holding out a hand to her. "Viv, this must stop. I've been thinking about us, the way I ended things between us…" He stopped, exhaled. "We need to talk."

She stumbled away. "No, we don't, Ghaleb."

It was only when she was feet away that her raw eyes encompassed the majestic sight he made in the moonlight. Everything about him abraded her. He'd changed back into Western clothes, was wearing a long black coat that flowed down his six-foot-five frame, making him look like a cross between a modern-day genie and the vampire she'd once likened him to.

"*Zain.* Fine." He inexorably eliminated the distance she'd managed to put between them. "I need to talk. You have to let me…"

"No. I don't have to let you do anything."

He only surged toward her, his intention to do what he'd withheld from doing so far, pulverizing her resistance, emblazoned on his brutally handsome face.

If he caught her, if he touched her, she'd be lost.

She stumbled backward, spun around and ran back to the only sanctuary she sensed he wouldn't invade—her tent—a snarl tearing from her. "I *won't* let you. Ever again."

# CHAPTER EIGHT

"NOW WE'VE EXAMINED the last, and in my opinion the most interesting case on our grand round," Viv said as soon as they were out of the patient's hearing. "Let's review his case. Lo'ai, sum up his history, please."

Ghaleb stood back, his arms folded on his chest, the only one in the crowd gathered for the weekly educational round whose eyes remained on Viv instead of moving to the resident. She, of course, didn't look at him. She'd stopped looking at him at all. She'd stopped talking to him, too. Even in public. For two weeks now. It was clear she'd meant "never again" in its literal sense.

But while she'd shut down with him, she'd become wide open with others, involved, rushing everywhere, her hand in everything. The only time he saw her still was when she was standing at her door, ready to be picked up at 7 a.m. sharp, her smile and greeting directed at Abdur-

Ruhman. She entered the limo, opened a book and buried her head in it. When forced to answer him, she gave monosyllabic answers. Then they arrived at the center and she hurtled into work with a ferocity he'd never encountered, not even with himself, the man everyone called driven. She stayed till late at night, and as he remained with her, he couldn't tear himself away except for necessary business. He hadn't seen Sam or Anna again since their camping trip. The schedule Viv kept, not the one he'd proposed, made sure of that.

All through it was as if he could see his old hyperactive Viv again, the flares of restless energy sizzling from her once placid surface. It had oppressed him, maddened him.

Until today. Until just now. He'd suddenly realized what all this was about. It was all a helpless reaction. To his presence. An act. To ward him off.

He was driving her as insane as she was driving him.

Had her old volatility been a reaction to him, too? An involuntary effort to keep his interest, even fear of losing it?

If that was the truth, as he now believed it was,

it no longer mattered what she said she wanted. They *would* talk.

His mind made up, he let his gaze linger on her one more second before moving to the one who was talking now, a smile of irony and satisfaction touching his lips when he felt her tension wind down the moment he relieved her from his focus. She was as painfully aware of him, with every breath, as he was aware of her.

"Es-Sayed Faisal Abulkhair, sixty-five, smoker," Lo'ai said, raising his head from his notes. "Current history began with an episode of loss of consciousness. His doctor ordered a chest CT that revealed an aneurysm at the aortic arch. The doctor then ordered coronary arteriography, which demonstrated obstruction of two branches. Left ventriculography demonstrated another aneurysm."

"Everyone got that?" Viv asked. Everyone made confirming noises. "Okay, I'll take comments and questions now."

"With a diagnosis reached after CT, why did the doctor order more investigations?" Ablah, their newest resident, asked.

Viv looked around. "Who can tell Ablah why?"

"Because a diagnosis was *not* reached. The

aneurysm didn't explain his fainting spell," Jamal, a third-year resident, said. He was talented, but it wasn't the first time he'd exhibited misplaced confidence and dangerously incomplete knowledge. Ghaleb made a mental note to have a serious talk with him, soon. "Aortic arch aneurysms are asymptomatic."

Viv looked around, her eyes falling on Aneesah.

"AAAs are *not* asymptomatic," Aneesah shot back. "The symptoms are so nonspecific that most doctors pursue other diagnoses before even thinking of them."

Viv nodded. "So why, since the aneurysm explained his symptoms, did the doctor pursue more investigations?"

"It's because the doctor dug into his file and found history of an old infarction," Aneesah said, looking at Ablah with the same nurturing care Viv regarded *her* with. "Leading to the suspicion his was a compound case and to more investigations."

Ghaleb's lips twitched at the undercurrent of feminine solidarity that had flourished since Viv's arrival. He liked it, and liked the results it was reaping. It had been a good decision to hire a woman for this position. It had turned out to be his best ever because it was Viv, whom he believed to be unequalled.

"Great question, Ablah," Viv said. "Perfect answer, Aneesah."

"That family doctor is a thorough man," Jamal said, trying and failing to defend his own sloppiness.

"*Woman.*" Aneesah smirked, drawing a chuckle from everyone.

"Indeed she was, on both counts." Viv smiled, too, before turning more serious. "She did exactly what we all should always do—never be satisfied with the first set of investigations giving us an explanation for a patient's symptoms. *Especially* if they corroborate our first diagnosis."

She let that sink in before adding, "Now Dr. Ghaleb and I will perform a total aortic arch replacement and a simultaneous ventricular patch plasty. If you don't have other pressing duties, I urge you all to come and observe."

Ghaleb came forward then, parting the throng gathered around Viv. "We come to the end of another great grand round, made far more stimulating by Dr. Vivienne." And he wasn't pandering to her in any way. She did make him realize he'd made his grand rounds drier and therefore less effective than they could have been. "Until another one next week, hit the books again. Most of you…" he gave Jamal a brief look he knew would keep him awake at night, as it should "…are doing better academically all the time. Keep it up."

Viv strode ahead at once, surrounded by chattering residents, some of whom stole looks back at him, no doubt wondering how it was possible for her to get away with treating him that way.

He started walking, too, returning the curious glances with a steely steadiness. He knew everyone was speculating on what was going on between him and Viv, could pick up on her pointed alienation. Hell, they probably got electrified every time they bumped into the field of tension that existed between them.

Not that anybody had dared make comments, even in the privacy of their own conversations. Adnan would have told him if tongues were wagging in the center.

Not that he cared. Let everyone talk. He didn't mind either that everyone witnessed Viv punishing him. He deserved it, and much more. He deserved anything, even to lose her. But he couldn't let it end this way. He wouldn't. He had to put things right. And he would, not because he couldn't live with the guilt, couldn't bear her alienation anymore, couldn't face the idea of a life without her. He would put things right for *her.*

It was time he took drastic action.

"Prince Ghaleb will not be riding home with you tonight, Doctorah Vivienne."

Viv looked up at Abdur-Ruhman, one thought echoing in her mind. *But Ghaleb always rides home with me.*

She nodded numbly, walked ahead out of the center, unable to digest the fact, still expecting Ghaleb to materialize beside her as he always did, stealing furtive glances around looking for him.

It was only when they were speeding down the highway that it sank in. Ghaleb really wasn't riding home with her.

Why hadn't he said anything after they'd finished their list? Did he have other things to do? In the center or at the palace? Maybe a matter of state? Or did he have a private engagement?

They'd finished early tonight. It was only eight. Was he now heading to a date? Date…What a lame, inappropriate word. Ghaleb wouldn't go out on dates but on conquests. On acquisition campaigns. Though Omraania was a strict society, and it was never talked about openly, it was accepted that rich men, especially royals, would keep mistresses, whom they kept in the lap of luxury. Ghaleb probably had his own harem.

She believed he hadn't been seeking his entertainment there since she'd arrived. Not with their long days and his focus on her, and with him not being one for rushed encounters. So had she succeeded in making him give up on her and he'd shrugged and moved on, was picking up where he'd left off?

If so, thank God she hadn't succumbed, hadn't let him take what he wanted, taking her apart again when he hadn't even wanted her enough to last three weeks before turning to other women.

She closed her eyes on the images of him bared to the hunger of another woman, maybe more than one at once, his magnificent body being worshipped, begged for.

She'd known she wouldn't last the two months. Just over three weeks had her teetering at breaking point. But now, God...*now.*

It was stupid and contrary of her, but she wouldn't bear being near him, knowing he'd just shared his body with another, found release and pleasure inside her. It was crazy to feel this way. He had no claim, never had had one, but she couldn't bear it.

Her breath hitched, her eyes burned. She fisted her hands, struggled to hold in the sobs accumulating inside her that were clamoring to burst out in a torrent of weeping. She couldn't let Abdur-Ruhman see her condition, couldn't show up with a blotched and swollen face when Anna and Sam were still awake, couldn't face their concern and questions.

She would end it tonight. She'd tell them they were going home. She expected dismay and efforts to change her mind. But she'd made it up. She had to be out of Omraania by morning.

She opened her eyes, turned her head on the headrest and looked out of the window. She stared at the total darkness outside for blank moments. Where had the highway, blazing with lights, and glittering Jobail gone?

It was a few more moments before the realization hit her.

This wasn't the way home. They were heading into the desert.

She turned to look out of the back window.

They weren't heading there, they were right in the *middle* of the desert.

So that was why they'd taken this monster four-wheel drive instead of the limo. This was premeditated.

She sat back for stunned moments, staring numbly at the back of Abdur-Ruhman's head across the bulletproof barrier. She wasn't even alarmed, she realized. She couldn't suspect Abdur-Ruhman of any wrongdoing. Which might be stupid, considering he was taking her into nowhere. But no—it wasn't stupid. She sensed nothing but goodwill from him. As always. So what was going on here?

She opened the radio channel between their compartments. "Why aren't we going home, Abdur-Ruhman?"

He didn't answer for a full minute.

Then he exhaled. "I'm following Prince Ghaleb's orders."

*Of course.* Why hadn't she realized that at once?

So he hadn't gone to one of his women...

Suddenly anger erupted—at herself, at him. "I demand that you take me back, Abdur-Ruhman. Immediately."

"Doctorah Vivienne, *ana khadamek,* but..."

"Spare me the *ana khadamek* bit, please," she snarled. "And just what does *khadamek* mean anyway?"

"It means I'm your servant."

"You're *not* my servant, Abdur-Ruhman," she grated.

"I *am,*" he insisted. "But—"

She cut him off. "But it's Ghaleb you obey. And you're taking me to him. You do realize I haven't agreed to go, right? That instead of being here himself, to take responsibility for his actions, he's assigned you to kidnap me?"

When he spoke again, his gruff voice sounded pained. "Forgive me if I'm causing you any distress, *ya doctorah.* I'd give my arm for you, but I'd give my life for Prince Ghaleb."

That deflated her. The poor guy had nothing to do with this, was just following the orders of an all-powerful master.

She should save her fury for said master.

When she said nothing more, Abdur-Ruhman talked again, this time sounding a little relieved that she seemed to accept the situation. "It'll be about two hours before we reach our destination, so maybe you'd like to get some sleep?"

Sleep. Yeah, right.

But maybe she should try to get some. To gain stamina for what lay ahead. What felt like the fight of her life.

She exhaled, made a conscious effort to relax all her muscles, slumped into a more comfortable position, squeezed her eyes shut and regulated her breathing...

The next thing she felt was a cool breeze on her face.

Her eyes snapped open, fell on Abdur-Ruhman.

He was standing outside her open door.

Man, she *had* slept. Like a log. And they'd arrived. Wherever Ghaleb had seen fit to bring her.

She waded through molasses-like lethargy and her heartbeat started to accelerate beyond the comfort zone.

She'd face Ghaleb now. She wasn't ready. She wanted to get it over with. She dreaded it. She couldn't wait for it.

*Just get out of the car and go and take that bastard apart!*

With that rallying cry ringing in her head, she staggered out of the car. Abdur-Ruhman made way for her but she sensed his reluctance to move away. She looked at him, saw the anxious look in his eyes and understood. He needed absolution from her.

She gave it to him. "It's all right, Abdur-Ruhman."

His huge body sagged with relief and he smiled for the first time that night. *"Rubbena yekremek, ya kareemah."*

"I'm not even going to ask what that means."

His smile broadened. "May God shower his generosity on you, generous one."

She smiled, too, accepting his prayer, even if she didn't agree with its claim. She wasn't generous, was barely trying to be fair here. But he'd see her this way. He was a good man.

Now she had a not-so-good man to see.

She cleared the barrier of Abdur-Ruhman's body and froze.

Barely a dozen feet away, Ghaleb was standing at the top of three-foot-wide stone steps leading to a columned patio that wrapped around a one-level lodge, the lights burning from the windows those of flickering flames, not electricity.

He was dressed all in white, his *abaya* billowing around him in the night wind like fog, like the ephemeral wings of a preternatural bird of prey, with him in the middle of the enchantment, every feminine fantasy come to life.

Then he spoke, his voice as deep, dark and heart-wrenching as the night desert around them. "Thank you, Abdur-Ruhman. I'll call you when I need you."

The big man gave his prince a solemn nod.

Just as he turned to leave, she shot him a "Ditto."

She could swear she saw him suppressing a grin.

The moment he drove away, she forced her wobbling legs to move, started toward Ghaleb. *He* wasn't smiling. He stood there, his gaze burning her, making her feel like he was giving her a total body scan, memorizing her down to her last cell.

She let the reaction he wrung from her fuel her anger with every breath. When she reached the bottom of the steps below him, she hurled it at him.

"So you indulge in criminal activities besides surgical and princely ones. I should have known. Being all-powerful here, you'd get away with murder. So what's a tiny thing like kidnapping?"

He smiled then. She didn't know how she remained on her feet with the eruption of rage, arousal and desperation.

He came down one step, then another, his

movements flowing, controlled, tranquil, as if he was afraid she'd bolt if he moved too fast. He reached a hand to her with the same care.

"Come in from the cold, Viv."

She avoided his hand, sidestepped him as she climbed the stairs. "Of course I will. You've left me no choice but to enter your—your…" She threw a hand at the dwelling every stiff step took her closer to. "What is this place anyway?"

"It's my hideaway."

She gave a ridiculing sniff. "One of your lairs. I see."

"Back to the predator motif?"

"You're playing to form."

"I didn't kidnap you, Viv."

"No, you made poor Abdur-Ruhman do it."

"I had to come ahead to prepare a few things. I came by helicopter, could have got you here the same way to save you the long trip, but you didn't like riding one to Az-Zaferah."

"How considerate of you. And, of course, kidnapping me by car had nothing to do with your fear that a helicopter would have exposed the little fact that I wasn't going home, causing me to resist, make a scene."

"I would have thought of something convincing to get you aboard peacefully. I didn't want you flying because it disturbs you, and I wouldn't have been there with you."

"So you would have only devised a more elaborate con to put me on a chopper, and I'm supposed to feel grateful that you considered my newfound fear of flight and spared me?"

"I'm not looking for gratitude, but I won't let you drag us into a new conflict. Even if you aren't here to make peace with me, I will make it, Viv."

"So this is how you negotiate your peace settlements? Hijacking your opponents' choices, or, as in this case, hijacking them themselves and cornering them into giving in to your version of harmony? The edition where you get your say, your way?"

And, damn him, his smile broke out again, even more bone-liquefying. A chuckle even rumbled deep in his chest.

"So glad to see you still think I qualify for your court clown position," she said bitterly.

He shook his head, made a visible effort to contain his mirth. "Your wit pushes buttons I didn't know I had, Viv. Everything you say exhilarates me. Or aggravates me. Any word that spills out of your mouth is guaranteed to get some unprecedented reaction from me." He raised a hand, stopping the retort she would have hurled at him. "But to prove to you that I do negotiate, yes, I admit I had to resort to kidnapping you. I had to give you no more chance to keep pushing me away and hiding behind work, or Sam and Anna."

"So, in effect, you're not admitting your guilt, you're just saying I made you do it, huh? How typically male."

"Are you being typically female, Viv? If you are, don't. You don't need this, can't possibly make me hungrier for you."

"What's 'this'? You think I'm playing games with you? You still don't believe I'm not here to pick up where *you* left off? Well, I *never* played games. If I ever had, if I knew how to play them, this wouldn't be my life. And just why are you hungry for me? Why the resurrected interest? *Because* you think I'm playing games? Well, I'm not. This is me, unadorned, and there's nothing intriguing about me."

A gust of wind changed direction and temperature, weaving out tendrils from her bun, invading the cotton of her shirt, sending a shudder cascading through her.

Ghaleb frowned. "I will not have a seven-year-overdue discussion out here when the temperature is forecast to drop to near zero. Come inside, Viv." He came a step closer.

She took a step back. "On second thoughts, no, I won't. I'll stay out here and risk hypothermia until you call Abdur-Ruhman back and tell him to take me to my family…" Her heart gave a terrible thud. "Didn't it occur to you to think how worried they'd be about me?"

He gave an easy shrug. "I told Anna you'd be with me."

"You told her…you…you…" She came to a stop under the pressure of her rage. Then she exploded. "*How dare you?* How *dare* you compromise me? How *dare* you make her think I'm…I'm…?"

"My lover? But you are, Viv."

She felt faint. There was nothing but air around her but she found none to draw into her lungs. She stared at him, towering above her, swathed in silk and starlight, at one with the overpowering surroundings, as pitiless as the night, as unattainable as the stars, weaving his irreversible spell as carelessly as they did.

How could he be so cruel? How dare he look

so convinced, sound so convincing as he uttered that lie?

A second before her lungs imploded, cold air forced its way into them, inflating them so suddenly she felt they'd burst.

She let out a hacked exhalation, letting her hiss ride its shaky thrust. "I *was*…in ancient history. And I *wasn't* your lover then, just one of the women who warmed your bed."

At that he advanced on her, inexorable, his face heart-snatching. She tried to stumble away. He only grabbed her arm, not roughly, just inescapably, bent, scooped her behind her knees, then she was swept up in his arms, held against his heat and hardness. It was as if he'd electrocuted her, sending her nerves firing in unison, paralyzing her.

He strode toward the house that looked like some mystical creature crouching in wait on the sands of the desert, its window eyes flaring and subsiding in barely checked hunger.

Her lips trembled as his gaze clung to them, reading her efforts to articulate the riot razing through her mind. All she could muster was a choked sound as he shouldered the door open.

And he muttered, "Save your breath for round two, Viv."

# CHAPTER NINE

WHAT BREATH?

That was all Viv could think as Ghaleb carried her inside.

He navigated through one arch after another in a corridor that made her feel he was taking her deeper into some wizard's sanctuary.

Which he was. He'd said this was his hideaway. And he'd always practiced magic. At least on her.

This place was as far as it could be from the opulent grandeur of every place she'd seen in Omraania, composed of all the elements of its nature, unpolished and unpretentious, and more evocative and atmospheric than the mind-boggling edifices for its simplicity and rawness.

He entered a hall with stone walls and adobe floors, strewn extensively with handwoven *keleems,* their same combination of colors draping cushions of every size smothering one long, low wooden settee. It rested against the wall with a square table traveling its length, spread in covered earthenware serving dishes on heating pedestals. A fireplace made of yet another mix of rocks flanked the sitting-cum-dining area, its flames leaping in a hypnotic dance, the only source of light in the place.

His hands on her changed pressure as he lowered her to her feet, each press, each gust of breath flaying her face. And he'd advised her to save her breath. She could barely draw in enough air to maintain consciousness, submerged in a will-draining well.

She had to accept his strength until she relocated a portion of her own. She leaned on him, looked sideways so she'd remove her face from his chest. "Another 'working' dinner?"

He gave her a tug toward the settee-table combination. "How about you eat before round two?"

"I'm not hungry." *Not for food, damn you,* she almost added.

He scowled down at her. "How can you not be? You haven't eaten since early this morning."

"I beg to differ. I ate two of those sinful *shawermah* sandwiches for lunch."

"I didn't see you eating."

"I should hope you didn't. I'd hate to think you could see me even when you're not there. You went to deal with a state matter. But, of course, since you didn't see it, it didn't happen."

"You've lost what must be ten pounds since you came here."

What had he done? Weighed her?

She tried to shrug it off. "I've been working hard."

That only intensified the displeasure darkening his face. "From what I now know, you've been working hard for the past seven years. Harder than anybody should have to."

An incredulous sound escaped her. "Not everyone is born with an oil state at their disposal."

Her barb slid right off him, his eyes gentling, something entering them. Cajoling? No. Beseeching…? Yeah, right.

"This isn't the first time you've made it clear you think I dip into the kingdom's funds, Viv," he said, his voice full of the same indefinable inflections. "I can prove to you that I don't but we're not talking about my status or the source of my wealth now."

"What are we talking about, then? Why did you bring me here? What do you want me to say?

What do you want to hear? That I'm losing weight over you?"

"Viv, you must stop doing this. Let me…"

She could no longer listen to him, desperation seeping through her.

She cut him off, her voice alien in her ears. "Will it satisfy you if I stop 'this'—resisting you or antagonizing you or whatever you think I'm doing? Will it appease you if I bow to your will like all others? Will you stop playing your games with me then?"

Urgency crowded his face as she spoke, translated into a tight step toward her, his hand reaching for her. "I'm not playing games, Viv. I never played games with you."

"Never?" The word punched out of her throat like a laser beam. She could almost feel it charring her flesh.

He dropped his hand to his side. "*Zain*—I admit at first the change in you, the turnabout in your behavior with me, did rouse the hunter that has lain dormant inside me all my life. I did want to conquer your antipathy. But that lasted only hours, until we had our dinner and I felt I was seeing the real you for the first time. But even until then I wasn't playing games, was only convinced you were."

"You always played games with me." She couldn't hold back the accusation, surrendered, let it out. "From the first day."

He looked startled at that. "You're talking about the past? But you were the one—"

"I was the one who pursued you? So I was. You could have turned me down, but you couldn't resist, could you?"

"No, I couldn't. Viv—"

"You couldn't resist taking all I offered as you toyed with me to see how far I'd go, even after you treated me like an indulgence you were ashamed of, even after you told me you'd leave at any time. Then you left without even a thank-you."

Something stark and bleak invaded his eyes. "Viv, that isn't what happened and we both know it."

"We do? Didn't you tell me, right before you took me that first time, right against my condo door, that you couldn't afford to have anyone know about us? And right afterward, when you were still inside me, you told me you'd have to go and fulfill your duties soon, and would never see me again?"

A hard-breathing silence followed her outburst, the mutilating memories she hadn't let herself access for so many years pouring out of her.

Then he muttered, his voice abraded, abrading, "I was in an untenable position. With my father ascending the throne after my uncle's death and me ascending to the crown prince's position, I had Omraania's image and reputation resting on my shoulders, and every eye was on me. Any misstep would have had widespread repercussions. I thought you understood, accepted it…"

"Oh, yes, I would have accepted anything to be with you. And you knew it, took full advantage of it. You saw me at that time, twenty-six going on sixteen, a mass of insecurities, making every disastrous choice, looking for warmth and acknowledgment from the only two men in the world who'd told me, to my face, not to expect them to treat me as human."

Suddenly he seemed to turn from flesh to granite. "If you're likening me to your father…"

"You're *worse* than him," she slashed at him, her control gone, the floodgates of bitterness and misery exploding. She bled. Gushed. Her life force jetting out of her with the released pain. "My father is a tiny man who's conned his way through life and I was what he believed would expose him for the fraud he is. When he lashed out, it was out of fear, out of loathing the very idea of my existence, something he'd never pretended not to feel. It was I who'd been clinging to the juvenile dream of an estranged father who'd come to his senses and admit he needed me as much as I thought I needed him. But you—you *knew* I posed no danger to you, you did take your pleasure with me, and you still chose to withhold even a smile as you walked away, left me without even the ability to hold on to whatever memories I thought we'd shared."

The hemorrhage suddenly stopped. She'd bled out and not a drop remained. She felt hollow, insubstantial. Finished.

It was really over now.

Ghaleb stared at Viv, every word that had poured from her lips like a scalpel of remorse gouging out another vital part of him.

He felt gored and gutted.

It didn't matter. Only she did. He needed to heal her pain, heal her wounds, bring life back into her eyes, restore her dignity. He'd pay any price, make any sacrifice.

"You have every reason to think me a heartless monster…" he started, only for his voice to shake away his efforts to leash it under control. It was moments of hacking silence before he could talk again. "I *was,* to treat you that way, no matter the reason. You gave me nothing but warmth and pleasure, and even if I heard you say I meant nothing to you, it still was no reason to—"

Some semblance of life came back into her eyes. They narrowed at him. "You heard me say that?"

This time he welcomed the detonation of pain at the clarity of the memory. "Yes."

After a hard-staring moment, she only said, "Good. I'm glad."

She was glad he'd been hurt, too. Or, according to her belief in his total lack of feeling, his ego had been. Suddenly clarity encompassed everything, slamming the truth into his mind.

"You didn't mean it." The fact almost choked him on the way out. "Why did you say it, then, Viv?"

"Why? Isn't that a belated question? What you should have asked right there and then? Why didn't you just get me alone and say, 'Viv, you said you loved me. I heard you say I mean nothing to you. Explain yourself.'"

He opened his mouth to confess how he hadn't wanted to hear what he'd believed would be lies.

She ploughed on, splintering his thoughts,

driving their jagged pieces into his heart. "I'll tell you why. Because you'd already made up your mind you wouldn't believe what I had to say. Because it was the perfect excuse for you to walk away without paying me the least acknowledgment, and you weren't going to blow it. But your ego still demands satisfaction, doesn't it? You want to know why I said that to that woman? The one who told me you'd been sleeping with her on the side? What did you want me to say to her when she taunted me with her knowledge of our so-called secret affair? That I loved you beyond reason? That I'd thrown self-respect—hell, self-*preservation*—to the winds to be with you, in secret, and as it turned out, not even exclusively, for a few weeks? What other answer could I have given her when I knew you'd leave and I'd suffer only ridicule and cruelty in your wake? What could I have done but borrow your own sentiments about me to ensure my survival among the people who knew us both after you left me alone among them?"

*That was it.* The explanation he'd *known* existed, that cleansed the last smudge on her shining image. The explanation that painted his soul black, made his sins irredeemable.

He'd known since the first night he'd met her again that he'd misjudged and mistreated her. By the time he'd met Anna again, he'd thought he'd realized the extent of both crimes. But that had been when he'd still believed what he'd overheard had had some truth to it. But now, *ya Ullah,* now…

*How could he live, knowing what he'd done to her? To them?*

She wasn't finished. "But you're telling me you left me, and that way, because of what you overheard? Because you were—what? Hurt? God, you're such a hypocrite. I, or what I felt for you, meant less than nothing to you. You were leaving anyway. You only found that the easiest way out, sparing yourself even a moment of discomfort on my behalf, probably even enjoying kicking me while I was down at your feet."

Suddenly he couldn't stand. More shame or guilt or agony. He wanted to fall at her feet, but she wouldn't want him there. She'd made it clear that nothing he could do would matter to her again. But he had to offer her all he could, a total admission of guilt, the power to exact whatever punishment she saw fit.

He leaned against the nearest wall before his

legs gave out. "I've sinned against you, Viv. I can't encompass the extent of how much I have. Women—people—always saw only what I represent, coveted only what I could offer, but you were the only person who never took anything from me while giving me all you had. Yet at the first doubt I judged you without a hearing, took out all my prejudice on you. I say this not to mitigate my guilt, just to state facts.

"It isn't true you meant nothing to me. You meant all that another person could have meant to me at that turbulent time in my life. You were so alive, so generous, I drowned in you, grabbed at everything you inundated me with. But every time I reminded you it was temporary, I was actually reminding myself, because I touched you and I forgot. Myself, my duties, the world. I was coming to ask you to come here with me. It was a crazy, unformed idea, but I couldn't bear leaving you behind. Then I overheard you. And you're right. I told myself I was hurt but I did grab at that way out. I convinced myself I owed you nothing, that I had to focus all I had on far more important things than you or what I felt for you. And though it makes nothing better, I swear to you I never looked at another woman the whole time we were together. I was exploitative, selfish, callous, but I did not two-time you. I was yours alone, Viv."

*I still am. I will always be.*

The pledge stuck unuttered in his heart, frozen there by the blankness of her stare. Silence descended, bore down.

She was the one who lifted it before it crushed him.

"I appreciate the explanations," she said in that efficient tone she used at work. "I can see now you had good reasons for doing what you did. I can only imagine what being you means, what kind of burden your status is, what it entails of alienation from all others through your inability to trust anyone's feelings and motives toward you. I can understand how overhearing another confirmation of your prejudices made you unable to give me the benefit of the doubt, even if that served your purpose. So, yes, I understand your reasons, but the outcome remains the same. Still, it's good you got it off your chest."

An ugly, self-loathing laugh was torn from him. "Off my chest? When I injured you so gravely? When I can never atone even if I spend my life trying to make amends?"

"What didn't kill me only made me stronger, so I should even be thanking you. As for amends, thanks, but, no, thanks, Ghaleb. I don't need them."

More pieces shattered inside him as overpowering love and tenderness swept through him with the force of a sandstorm. "I know you don't need them. Or me. You've become a marvel, Viv. You're the strongest person I've ever known."

"I don't know about *the* strongest, but I'm okay." She straightened into an about-to-end-a-conversation posture. "I trust we've said all there is to say, aired all grievances, made apologies, gave absolution and commendations and all that. I'd say the peace you wanted to make with me is well and truly made now."

He stepped into her path as she made to move. "Are you at peace now, Viv?"

She looked up with those empty eyes. "That's another belated question, Ghaleb. I may have thought I needed peace then, that the way to get it was through somebody else, but I'm long beyond such illusions. Now I have all I need— Sam, Anna, and the purpose and ability to give them the best life possible."

"What about *you*, Viv?" he insisted.

"I'm fine, too. Thanks for asking."

She walked on then. He didn't stop her this time, just watched her as she extracted her phone, desperation roiling inside him.

He'd fooled himself yet again. He'd staged tonight for her, but he *had* been hoping for some kind of reconciliation, to salvage his own life, too. Now one last hope remained.

"You said you loved me."

The statement came out as a plea, for a stay of execution.

She only looked up from her phone for a second and shrugged. "And love dies. You've killed anything I felt for you, Ghaleb, no matter your reasons. So put your mind to rest on that account, too."

She thought he was worried that lingering emotions for him tormented her, was telling him none remained. Good or bad.

If she'd spoken those words with any of her previous fervor or agitation or sarcasm, he would have launched into all-out efforts to convince her that though he hadn't deserved her love before, he'd live the rest of his life doing so now. But with her eyes clear and her tone steady, the conviction, the finality in her words was a guillotine blade falling.

He'd existed without her when he'd had something to cling to, a lie he'd wanted to believe so he could go on. Now there'd be nothing without her. This was an end of hope. All reason to live.

All reason, period.

He moved toward her, propelled by survival, the growl that was torn from him that of a mortally wounded lion.

"You still want me."

She looked up, startled, her finger freezing on the call button. He saw Abdur-Ruhman's number on the screen as he took the phone from her. Then he advanced on her.

She moved away, each step back retracing the ones he'd taken when he'd brought her here a lifetime ago. She ended up plastered against the lodge door. He didn't crush her against it as every nerve fiber was screaming for him to, praying she'd say something, change her verdict, his sentence…

"Are you going to keep me here against my will?"

He flinched. "Don't, Viv. I don't deserve any mercy but…*don't.*"

"Please, let me go."

He looked down into her eyes and knew. This was it. He'd long lost her love and faith. Now he'd lost the last measure of her respect or good opinion. He'd lost everything.

His shoulders slumped in final defeat.

He handed her back her phone. "If you'd rather take the chopper back, Abdur-Ruhman will arrange it. I'm turning the center over to you. I won't be coming in again. I hope you can forgive me one day."

He turned away, feeling cut wide open.

"Ghaleb…"

The velvet of her voice caressed his name, lodged between the shoulder blades with the force of an ax.

"I still want you."

# CHAPTER TEN

GHALEB LURCHED AS IF he'd been hit by lightning.

He'd been slowly building up to a breakdown for years now. Was this it? Was he having delusions? While awake?

The words, not the ones he needed to survive but still far more than he deserved, than he dreamed of, looped in his mind.

*I still want you.*

He turned to look at her.

She was still leaning back against the door, her eyes flaring and subsiding with golden fever in the dimness.

In a trance he walked back to her, careful not to make any sudden moves, afraid this dream might come to an end, as every tortured, torturing one had in the past seven years.

When he was a foot away, she did something that stopped his heart. What she'd done that day in her condo seven years ago.

She raised her arms above her head, arched in invitation, in surrender, a scorching moan spilling from her lips.

A groan shredded out of his starving depths in answer as he obeyed her unspoken command, uncoordinated hands bunching in the edge of her sweatshirt.

But instead of tearing it over her head, like he'd done that first time, the rest of her clothes following, only enough of his undone to press his flesh against hers, to free him to plunge inside her right there and then, he fell to his knees before her, buried his face in her exposed midriff, her imprisoned breasts, letting out a keen of longing and remorse, of agony and relief.

He mashed his face into the vitality, the privilege of her, inhaled her uniqueness, everything that made life worth living.

*"Please."*

The distress in the wavering word snapped his every hyper-extended nerve. Dreading he'd misunderstood somehow, that she'd changed her mind, that he was making her hate him even more, he looked up at her, begging, needing to know what she wanted, what she'd allow him. Her fingers flailed through his hair. He thought she'd push him away.

She only pulled his head back to her as she writhed for him, pressing her flesh into his lips, his hands, sanctioning all. Then hunger and urgency made sound poured certainty over him.

"I *want* you, Ghaleb."

Elation detonated inside him. He rained kisses all over her stomach, anywhere he could reach. "*Aih, ya habibati,* want me, *atawassal elaiki*—I beg you. I'm yours to want."

"Ghaleb…kiss my lips, give me yours…"

He heaved up, freed, given every license to pleasure her. He would take every one, drain each of every drop of abandon.

He devoured her lips, as she'd demanded, in his mind, as his hands shook her hair free from its imprisoning bun, speared into its luxury, cupped the shape and weight of her head as if cupping happiness itself. His heart stampeding, he ran shaking fingers over her face, inching nearer the fount of her taste, of his enslavement, until his fingertips luxuriated in every dimple of lips gasping for his. Then he froze.

He'd fantasized about this for so long, with such

ferocity, he was afraid. He wanted to be gentle, to be patient. He felt unrestrained, volcanic.

She dragged his head down to hers, surging up to crash her mouth against his. Her tongue delved inside his mouth, tangling in abandon with his. For stunned heartbeats he drowned in the shock of her taste, so acutely remembered yet so much more potent than memories, than fantasies. He let her storm him, let her show him the measure of her pent-up craving and impatience.

Then he took over.

He'd show her seven years' worth of hunger. Then he'd give her satiation well worth the wait.

He growled long and deep as he applied more pressure until she whimpered, opened fully, her hands clenching around his neck, her breasts pressing harder into his chest, cushioning him, one leg winding around his hip in a mind-blowing gesture of abandon. She was showing him she wanted anything he'd do to her. Anything at all.

Only when her undulations against him became frantic did he suckle her lip inside his mouth, in long, smooth pulls, drawing more plumpness into her succulent flesh, moving to her upper lip, alternating, running his tongue inside them, drawing more of her taste until her whimpers became incessant. Only then did he plunge, tongue and ferocity, drank her until he drained her, until she sagged in his hold with overstimulation.

He tore his lips from hers, trailed them over her cheek, jaw, neck, latched teeth and tongue there and nibbled, suckled, struggling to come down. He'd almost climaxed just kissing her, just imitating the craved possession with their mouths.

"Touch me, Ghaleb, all over… Let me touch you…"

"*Amrek, ya rohi*—command me…" He raised her arms over her head once more and in a luxurious upward sweep, freed her from her sweatshirt. Then he obeyed her, his hands roving over her, everywhere at once, down her arms, her back, her abdomen, over hot, silken skin and toned muscles, strength and femininity made woman, his woman, all the while kissing and suckling his way down from her hands to her armpit to her breasts through her bra.

She shuddered, squirmed. "Touch me, kiss me there…"

Elation fizzed higher in his blood. She'd never been vocal with him during lovemaking, never told him what she wanted.

"*Aih, gulili aish betridi*—tell me what you want, *ya galbi*." His voice shook, as his hands did over the fastening of her bra, shedding it with a flick, taking the weight of her in his palms. He stared at the ripened perfection of her, wondered if she'd breast-fed Sam, saw her breast-feeding another baby—his. The white-hot image seared into his mind with a longing that threatened to dismantle his soul. He groaned with the dread, the bleakness that it might never come to pass.

But this wasn't time to surrender to his fears and pain. This was her time.

He stroked her turgid flesh in wonder, squeezed the incredible resilience, his trembling fingers circling the buds he'd tasted during so many rides to ecstasy, thicker, darker now, and much more mouthwatering. "*Ma ajmalek, ya habibati, ajmal men zekrayati, men ahlami.*"

"What are you *saying?*" she moaned, as she turned her lips into any part of him she could reach, burying hot kisses into his neck, chest, arms, hands. "You never talked in Arabic before…"

He realized he never had. Realized he did now because he'd let go of all inhibitions and considerations, was true to her and to himself.

"I'm marveling at your beauty, so much more beautiful than my memories, my dreams."

She moaned, sank her teeth in his shoulder. "*You're* beautiful, the most beautiful thing I've ever seen…besides Sam. In—in a different way… you know…"

She choked and he moaned. "Stop, Viv. I can't take more now. Tell me later, *ya hayati.* I can't stand it now…"

With his tremors gaining momentum, he peeled off the utilitarian pants that wreaked havoc on his libido. Once he had her down to her white panties, she attacked his clothes. He let her push the *abaya* off his shoulders, let it drop to the floor, rocked to his foundations at the evidence of her desire while she bunched his buttonless shirt up and latched trembling hands and lips on the bursting muscles of his abdomen and torso. Growling, he held the shirt at the neck and ripped it in two. She cried out at the violence of his move, the sight of his body, flung herself at him, writhing against him as if she'd mingle their flesh. He roared as her greed for him spread over his flesh in kneading grabs and openmouthed bites. But when her hands went to the string fastening of his loose pants, his hand clamped them.

This wasn't about his pleasure. This was about hers.

He told her. *"Bareed amata'ek, ashaba'ek*—I want to pleasure you, sate you. Let me, *ya hayati."*

He went down on his knees before her again, taking her panties down in the same downward sweep, exposing her. Unable to take in more of her beauty, to stand more blows of arousal hammering in his blood, pounding in his loins, he closed his eyes, sculpted her in a frenzy of memory and wondrous rediscovery. Her flesh hummed beneath his fingers, boosting the electricity arcing there to unendurable levels.

*"Ghaleb*—don't make me wait anymore, don't hold back…" Her gasp was a strained thread of sound about to snap, blanking his mind with carnality.

He stormed up, devoured her pleas in a mouth turned ferocious, unleashed now he knew only the savagery of his need would satisfy her.

When she was flailing, his lips relinquished hers, razed a path of sensual exploitation lower, until they possessed her breasts, rained bites over their engorged beauty until she crushed his head to her, mashing her flesh into his mouth. He latched on one nipple then the other, alternating heavy pulls and sharp nips, each rewarded by a lurch and a cry.

When he felt her coming apart with stimulation, his hands dragged over her flesh down to her core. He spread her, slid between her feminine lips, almost blacked out with the extent of her readiness. Needing to be inside her, to feel her close around him, capture him, any part of him, to wallow in the freedom, the privilege, he probed her, plunged two then three long fingers into her scorching channel.

She screamed into his mouth. He jerked, afraid he'd hurt her, tried to snatch his hand away. Her thighs clamped it, her hands digging into him as her body convulsed, her sharp, spasmodic screams gusting into his mouth.

*She was climaxing. With but a touch.* The realization made him blossom with delight, with pride. He'd aroused her that much.

He allowed himself a moment to watch her in the throes of satisfaction, the sight he'd been starved of for seven bleak years. Then he took her mouth again, doing to it what his fingers had done to her core, plunging deeper, stretching her wider, feeding her frenzy, drawing out her satisfaction, loving every jerk, drinking every last whimper.

She slumped in his arms, precious weight and satisfied woman.

Or so he thought. In a minute her nails dragged down his back, her lips latched on one nipple, her leg rubbing against him, seeking his hardness. He almost jumped out of his skin when he felt her touch circling the head of his erection, slick in his own arousal. He looked down, found himself straining against his abdomen, half out of his pants.

He imprisoned her leg in both of his, clamped her hand. She slithered from his hold, subsided to her knees before him. "I want to touch you, Ghaleb, taste you…"

The sight alone, of her bowed head at his loins, her hair raining to one side, exposing her curves, the sweep of her back, the flare of her hips as she moved sinuously up and down, rubbing herself against his legs like a feline in heat, almost made him come.

"No." He dragged her up, crushed her to the door, mouth and body. "Later, Viv. Own me later. First…*areed aklek, akhullusek*—I want to devour you, finish you."

"No…just come inside me…" she protested. Urgent, tight. She climbed him, wrapped her legs around his hips, ground her moist heat over his erection. He surrendered to the torture, lapping up every show of need, then took hold of her hips, raised them as he went down, ending up with her legs draped over his shoulders, her back plastered to the smoothness of the door.

"*Daheenah ashba, w'ashaba'ek*—now I sate myself, and you. Viv, *rohi, hayati,* open yourself to me…"

She did, sagged in his hold, giving it all up to him.

He still couldn't believe he had her this way, open to his gaze, his pleasuring. After what he'd done to her, he didn't deserve the honor, the mercy. It was humbling that she desired him, as much as before. No, more. He could feel it. Her desire had grown stronger, as his had. But his passion had intensified with maturity, with the strength gained through the years, through knowing who he was and what really mattered, through the forging fires of denial and disappointment, frustration and separation, pain and loss. Mostly by total, unconditional love. Why had hers strengthened? He couldn't tell, could only give thanks.

He opened her folds, let his breath blow over the engorged bud of her arousal, drawing her mewls, her prodding scratches. He groaned in pleasured pain, obeyed her, took her feminine lips in a voracious kiss, his tongue lapping her in long sweeps. When her breath fractured, her pleas rose, he took her bud in and sucked. She thrashed, begged, incoherent. He tongued her faster. When he knew she couldn't stand any more, he bit down on her at the exact point where all her nerves converged.

She convulsed so hard, howled so piercingly that the shock went through his body, almost triggering his release. He again pushed three fingers inside her, sharpening her pleasure, lapping up its flood until her voice broke and her body collapsed.

He held her up, still lapping at her, soothing now, his head between her beloved thighs, tenderness a rising tide through the sustained agony, gratitude and pride sweeping him that he could pleasure her this way.

In minutes she stirred with a jerk and her hands were pulling at his hair. She wanted to be let up. He obeyed, enfolding her, felt the thrum of satiation echoing in her.

She dragged his head down, gave him a kiss bent on extracting his soul, her hands roaming his body, kneading, needing again.

She suckled his earlobe, bit it, sending a million arrows lodging into his erection, whispered in a voice roughened by abandon and satisfaction, "*Now* will you come inside me?"

He tried to pull away, took her hand. "*Enti to'-morini*...just command me. But let me take you to bed, replenish your desire."

She pulled him back, leaned on the door, raised her arms over her head again in that memory-triggering pose. "My desire can't be replenished more than that. I need you. Now. Here. *Here,* Ghaleb."

She wanted to re-enact their first time? Was it not too loathsome a memory, then?

His heart lifted in his chest at the implications.

Was there hope after all?

Yes, as long as breath powered his body, he'd create hope. Then he'd use every breath to make it take root, flower, last.

He moved on her, undulated against her, his hands reclaiming her secrets as he started—to her vigorous protests—slowly stoking her fire. She might be ready again, her accumulated desire still unfulfilled, but he didn't want her ready. He wanted her desperate, for his assuagement, his invasion, wanted his possession of her to be ecstasy with the first glide of his flesh into hers, had to have fulfillment shatter her, leave her unable to want again. For more than minutes this time.

Her hands flailed over him, creating erogenous zones wherever they landed, her lips spreading moans and gasps, explosions of stimulation over his body, hurtling him toward the point of no return.

He held back, sought evidence of her equal distress. He found it, in the madness of her heartbeat, the tremors of her core. He withdrew his hands, clamped them over the perfection of her buttocks, spread her.

She tried to help him, but she was coming apart, gave up, let him support her, wind her legs around him. Her eyes held his as he held her suspended above him, stormed through him with emotions that churned like an ocean-wide vortex, swallowing him whole.

*"Take me…"*

He'd intended to lower her onto him, let her take him. That plea sabotaged his intentions.

He thrust up into her, invading her molten honey, sheathing himself inside her to the hilt in one savage stroke, hurtling home, his only home. Her scream felt as if it was tearing with his own roar from his lungs. He wasn't fazed this time. This was pure pleasure, as his bellow had been. Her scream merged into others as she spasmed around him, her inner muscles wrenching at his length in a fit of release. He rode the breakers of her orgasm, withdrawing and plunging in a fury of rhythm, feeding her frenzy, until her heart accelerated into the danger zone, her tears pouring so that he feared he might be doing her real damage.

"Come with me…"

Her sob as her seizure continued around him broke his dam. He let go, buried himself in her, wished he could bury all of himself inside her, and surrendered to the most violent orgasm he'd ever known, jetting his essence into her depths in gush after excruciating gush, roaring his love, his worship.

*"Ahebbek ya hayati, ya rohi…Viv, aabodek…"*

Following the cataclysm, he felt the plateau of pleasure would never subside, that this was now what powered him, that he couldn't separate from her and survive it. He had to have her like this always, owning him, inside and out, pleasured, her flesh quaking with aftershocks, her sweat cooling… *Cooling?*

He staggered with her wrapped around him, reached his bedroom. He eased her back on the mattress on the floor, careful not to disturb their merging. His heart fired as her legs rubbed his buttocks, widening to accommodate him, showing him she couldn't bear separation either. But it was seeing her in the firelight, the goddess she'd become, reading surrender and satiation in her for-once unguarded features that almost finished him.

He filled her arms, made his pledge to the fates.

If he couldn't have her love, he'd wallow in her desire, fulfill her every need, lavish all his love and trust and honor on her. He'd keep her hungrier for more still, keep her beside him.

And one day, one day he'd resurrect her love.

Viv felt Ghaleb come over her, filling her arms, his expression as he drove deeper into her, as if he couldn't bear to be outside her, snapping the tethers of her heart. His weight and bulk became the gravity holding her universe together. The universe that had spun out of control when he'd turned away in that corridor, telling her she wouldn't be seeing him again.

She'd lost her mind in the eruption of fear. The truth had torn aside inhibitions, rationality, even survival, had burst out of her. At her admission he'd turned to her, shown her how he wanted her, but that it was her decision. As it had always been.

And she'd discovered the years hadn't changed a thing. She still needed him beyond self-preservation. She'd thrown herself into the heaven and hell of his arms again…

Now she felt herself falling into an endless spiral, everything dimming.

It felt like another life when she felt everything surging back. She opened her eyes that felt glued shut, found him lying on his side, his legs encompassing her, his head propped on one hand, the other sweeping her in caresses. This wasn't the position she last remembered. Which meant one thing.

"How long have I been out?" Her voice was thickened, sultry. The voice of a woman who'd been thoroughly, savagely pleasured. She did feel gloriously sore, every cell shrieking with life.

"An hour or so," he teased, reminding her of the time she'd fallen unconscious all over him on her first day in Omraania. "I love knowing I can knock you out with pleasure."

"Anything I can do for your male ego."

He hugged her exuberantly, before pulling back, his eyes turning serious. "You're right about male ego. Mine is all tied up in my ability to satisfy you, Viv. And now I know I do, I won't let you fight our need anymore. We must and will be together."

She closed her eyes, warding off the intensity in his.

It did nothing to reduce the brutality of temptation. She couldn't resist him or her need for him. But she had to protect herself. In every way. Though she wasn't in her fertile period, she'd take the morning-after pill to be sure, be religious about contraception this time. There was no way she could risk history repeating itself. And she'd lay down limits before Ghaleb swallowed her whole again.

She'd already complicated the situation beyond imagination by succumbing to the raging desire between them. She couldn't let this be open-ended, as he was proposing. He'd get married, and she couldn't be his mistress, as he must want her to be. This time she'd end it herself. She'd give herself the rest of her contracted two months in Omraania with him. And once their liaison came to an end, amicably this time, she'd tell him about Sam, discuss his future.

He kissed her eyes, prodded her. "Say yes, *ya mashoogati.*"

She opened her eyes, inhaled a shaky breath. "As long as we understand what this is about. Need and sexual fulfillment." She felt him stiffen. He took issue with her stripping their liaison of any emotional involvement. At all, or on her part? What would he do with hers? It was something he could never reciprocate, a complication he couldn't afford. Was it just male ego again?

She pulled out of his arms, lay on her back, unable to look at him as she laid out the terms of the liaison *she* could afford. "I'll be your lover again until my time here is up."

He poured obsidian displeasure over her, his jaw clenched on…what? Affront that she should talk to him this way? Frustration that he couldn't do anything about it?

"You're timing need and sexual fulfillment, Viv? What if by the end of the remaining five weeks you still need me? Still need the sexual fulfillment I provide?"

"I have a job to return to, Ghaleb. Sam has a school to go back to. If, after five weeks, our situations allow that, we can arrange to be together again when possible."

His gaze scoured her, until she was about to back down. At the last moment he was the one who looked away, his jaw working.

He disentangled her completely, stood up on the mattress, fully aroused. Giving her an eyeful of what she'd be losing when she walked away?

Oh, she knew what she'd be losing.

"Fine, Viv. Whatever you say. But here are my terms. I said we will be together, and we will be. You'll all stay with me in my summer palace by the sea. We'll commute to work by helicopter."

She opened her mouth and he pressed on. "That's not up for negotiation." Then he turned and strode to the en suite bathroom. In seconds she heard him running a bath.

She lay listening to his every move, desolation suffocating her. She'd convinced him she no longer loved him, could never love him again. She'd freed him to accept her temporary offer again with a clear conscience. Good for her. She'd only managed to destroy the barrier she'd erected to hide behind, to stop from facing the truth so she'd be able to function.

She loved him.

But she'd known that all along, barriers, self-evasions and all. There was something new now. Something far worse.

Now her love made her younger one pale into nothing.

Now she would never stop loving him.

Numb with self-confrontation, she watched him as he re-entered the room, went limp as he swooped down on her, scooped her up in his arms, making her feel as if she weighed nothing and headed to the bathroom.

"Ghaleb, about staying with you…"

His tongue drove hotly inside her mouth, stemming her words. "You'll be with me every minute. You will share my bed every night, and I will take every opportunity during the day to tend to your…need. Speaking of which, *ya galbi…*" He engulfed one nipple, suckled. She arched in instant surrender.

Her amazement soared as her body pounded at her, demanding his. She moaned, gasped. "After all you did to me, how can I want you again so soon?"

His onyx eyes glittered down on her, heavy with elation, with triumph, with voracity. "Because you won't ever get enough. Because you can't ever stop wanting me."

# CHAPTER ELEVEN

"This is the best place on earth!"

Viv cast an aching glance at Sam as he pirouetted with arms wide open as if to embrace the perfection around him, and had to admit he was right. This place *was* the best place on earth. It had all the people she loved in it.

Ghaleb had prevailed. He'd brought them to his summer palace the very next night.

Anna was by then certain what was going on between them but contrary to Viv's own desolation, Anna was ecstatic. She thought Ghaleb the most perfect man ever created and who but him suited her perfect Vivienne? She thought theirs was the romance of their era. Unable to bear her raptures, Viv explained to her the nature of their temporary arrangement, that Ghaleb wasn't a man who could choose the woman he loved. Not that he loved her. She made *that* abundantly clear.

Anna was unconvinced, thought it was Viv

who couldn't see clearly, and carried on in determined jubilation.

If not as much jubilation as Sam. Even after she explained that this was a vacation that would last only five weeks, he was unfazed. He said he'd hate to go back after it was over, but he was just happy Ghaleb had offered it. Wasn't Ghaleb the greatest guy on earth? And couldn't she marry him, please?

She explained Ghaleb's position to him and was stunned by his reaction. He was all solemn understanding. Princes had duties. And Ghaleb was the best prince in the world.

That gave her hope that when it was over between her and Ghaleb, Sam wouldn't feel bitter about it, wouldn't let it come between him and whatever relationship Ghaleb could afford to forge with him.

Ghaleb seemed to be constantly high. Working with her by day, spending his evenings with the three of them, then making love with her all through the night certainly agreed with him. She'd never seen him so relaxed, so elated, so heartbreakingly vital and beautiful.

In this idyll she was the only one reeling, her footing long lost, the waves of circumstances,

Ghaleb's actions and her love for him and Sam tossing her around.

Then, after the first week, something happened.

She was coming down to dinner after an afternoon spent making languorous love with Ghaleb. He'd gone down ahead of her.

As she neared his "family" room, she heard his laughter, the sound as always sending her nerve endings awry. She heard Anna's laughter, too. She approached, but something stopped her from making her presence known to them. She stood outside the door and watched as Sam reenacted a part of his favorite cartoon for his captive audience. He finished and hurtled into Ghaleb's arms, who received him with as much enthusiasm, showering him with praise, then turned to coaching him into fine-tuning his performance for when he would surprise her with it.

She again marveled at how Ghaleb had mastered a boy of Sam's infinite energy and inquisitiveness, secured his affection and commanded his respect. Just like he had the undying allegiance of a discerning woman like Anna, along with that of a whole nation.

Sam was flourishing under his influence and guidance, with Ghaleb patient yet responsive, firm yet indulgent, while Anna was glowing with contentment under his care and affection.

She knew at that moment he'd never tried to use Anna and Sam to get to her, that when she told him about Sam, he'd do everything in his power to make him happy.

Feeling that Sam's future would be secure, she no longer cared about her own. She decided there and then that for the next four weeks she would not think beyond the minute she was living with those who were her world.

She entered the room at that point and it was the first magical evening of what followed. Then came the nights of escalating abandon now she'd let herself love him with all she had, withholding nothing but the words.

From the moment she'd let herself go, their encounters had left them both devastated. That first time it had happened, he'd lain slumped on top of her, accusing her of devising yet another method of assassinating him, through a pleasure overdose, joking about registering her as a lethal weapon.

He could talk.

She now rose to watch Sam as he hurtled toward his new friend, Ahmad, Abdur-Ruhman's son, who was calling him to start flying their kite. They raced together, with Abdur-Ruhman following across the white sands that spread from the last step of the expansive circular west-facing veranda to the dunes.

It was a balmy Friday and she and Ghaleb had stayed in bed making love till two hours ago when she'd left him and come down to be with Sam and Anna. Anna had left to take her siesta and the sun was now blazing on its descent to the horizon, its angle deepening the azure waters to royal blue.

She hugged her arms around herself, raised her face to the wind. This was magic, this time they were living. But there was one more week left of it. And though she knew it was hopeless, loving Ghaleb far more deeply knowing how it would end sooner or later, she wasn't ready to end it any sooner than she had to. She couldn't. He'd been right. Five weeks were a drop of water when she was dying of thirst. One more week felt like a death sentence.

No. She couldn't end it, would have this, would let them all have this. For as long as it lasted.

Then, when it ended, the memories, rich in ecstasy and perfection this time, would fuel her for her desolate life ahead…

"What is *roh galbi* thinking?"

His words wrapped around her a second before his powerful arms did. She immediately leaned into him, felt him hardening for her as she turned her face to him readily, drowned in his perpetual desire, the heat of his appreciation. He kissed her anywhere now, overtly displaying the nature of their deeply erotic relationship.

The first time he'd caressed her at work, right in front of everyone, she'd been horrified. In answer to her horror, he'd pulled her into his arms and into a lingering kiss. As she'd sputtered and almost died of embarrassment he'd put his arm around her shoulders and walked her out of the center, meeting everyone's eyes serenely. Once in the back of the limo, he'd surrendered to her lambasting with a devilish grin.

When she'd exhausted herself and he'd again overcome her common sense, he'd looked down at her, a puddle of longing in his arms, had whispered against her lips, "I'm a pushing-forty lord of all I survey, *ya hayati*. My conservative people and my status are for me to worry about. Trust me to know what I'm doing."

She'd accepted that. It *was* his call. This was his country. He was the one whose reputation and position were at stake here. He must know he wasn't jeopardizing either. As for her, she'd be gone one day, sooner if not later…

*"Prince Ghaleb."*

The shout ripped the air, tearing them apart, sending them swinging around to its origin.

It was Abdur-Ruhman. He looked as if he'd seen a ghost.

Before either of them could ask anything, he wailed, "It's Sam. He slipped on the rocks in the western bay. He's unconscious, bleeding."

In the nightmare that had torn her world apart, Viv found herself, wading in what felt like quicksand, acid tears pouring from her eyes, eating into her face.

In the cacophony blaring in her mind she heard the rumblings of urgent thunder.

"Med chopper. To my summer palace's western bay. *Now.*"

Urgency pulled at her brain, barbed tentacles yanking through the fraying tissues. Before she understood what it was, the thunder was explaining the urgency, fulfilling it.

"Emergency bags. All of them. And the Jeep."

She kept running, Sam's name looping on shrill

snatches of sound. Suddenly she was swept off her feet, saw Ghaleb's face inches from hers, eyes grim, closed. She struggled. *"Ghaleb..."*

He restrained her, ran with her in his arms to intercept the Jeep. Then they were inside and hurtling closer to where her world lay bleeding away.

"Viv, listen to me. I want you to let me take care of Sam—"

"No...*no*..."

Ghaleb clamped her head in both hands, stopped her ferocious head shaking. "I understand what you're feeling..." She tried to shake her head again. "Yes, *I do.* If I can love Sam like I do, if I am this terrified, I *can* imagine how you feel. But if you can't stop being a frantic mother and be a doctor, I can't use you. I won't let you near him in this condition. Do you understand, Viv?"

Something clicked inside her mind, turning off the cacophony.

In the stillness that followed, she heard her voice, steady, resolute. "I'm fine. I will see to him. He's...everything..."

Ghaleb's black eyes probed her, then an exhalation bled from him. "We don't know how badly he's hurt yet. But, whatever it is, if you feel yourself slipping back into panic, step aside and leave him to me. Say yes, Viv."

She looked into his eyes, saw the rocklike steadiness, the infinite power. The sheer terror. And she knew she could trust him with much more than her life. With Sam's. She nodded.

The moment the car stopped, they leaped out.

She saw him at once. Hundreds of feet away. Sam. Lying over the rocks, on his back, the string of the kite tangled in his limp hand, the kite flailing on the water's surface. A few feet from him stood Ahmad, his small shoulders heaving, tears running down his face.

Hysteria bubbled to the surface again. She fought it down. If she'd ever needed to be strong, it was now. She had to be there for Sam. Couldn't let Ghaleb exclude her from fighting for her baby.

She ran, but love and terror were no match for Ghaleb's speed. He reached Sam a minute before she did, swooped down on him. Abdur-Ruhman reached Ahmad, scooped him up. They left her consciousness the moment they did her field of vision.

As she threw herself on Sam's other side, Ghaleb looked up at her, his face ablaze with anxiety mingled with relief.

"The bleeding is just a scalp wound. It has already stopped. His pulse is steady, his breathing unimpeded. His pupils are equal and reactive. All good signs." Ghaleb threw the emergency bags which Abdur-Ruhman had brought open. "No need to intubate. I'll check him over. You take circulation."

She nodded, her eyes wide on Sam, the feeling of wading into a surreal nightmare returning. He looked as if he was sleeping. Only in a pool of his own blood. The memory of her panic on their first night in Omraania, when she hadn't been able to wake him at once, flashed into her mind. Now she really couldn't wake him up.

Blindly, she bent and touched her lips to his cheek. Warm. Breathing tranquil. A sob went through her.

*"Viv."*

Ghaleb's warning galvanized her. She reached for a saline bag, giving set and needle, and gritted her teeth as she located a vein in Sam's arm and inserted the needle there. In minutes she had a drip going.

Then, with Ghaleb guiding her through the gaps terror had eaten through her medical knowledge, they examined Sam, concentrating on his neurological status.

At last Ghaleb sat back on his heels, capturing her chin, drawing her gaze away from Sam. "Apart from his loss of consciousness, he seems fine. No signs of intracranial or epidural hemorrhage. I suspect a severe concussion, but nothing beyond that." He flicked a glance at his watch. "The med chopper will be here in minutes. Until it arrives and we get to the center to get confirming CT and MRI scans, he's stable. You get him covered and warmed up while I suture his scalp wound."

"No, I'll do it…"

His hand was back on her, cupping her cheek, gentleness incarnate, his voice imploring, inexorable. "No, Viv. Let me do this, for both of you."

Her breathing fractured again. He was as entitled as she was to fight for Sam. And he wanted to. And it didn't feel like anything she'd felt from him before, the way he always wanted to fight for any patient. It felt as if he wanted to fight for Sam as if he was his. She looked into his eyes for final confirmation, found it blazing there.

Love. He loved Sam. Even thinking he was another man's child, he still loved him. It made him an even better man, a better father than she could have ever imagined.

And she still couldn't tell him. Not now. It had to be over between them before she could tell him. It almost made her change her decision not to leave next week.

But she couldn't. She *loved* him. Loved them both. Was too weak, too selfish. She needed to have more time with them both, as a pseudo-family, before it was over. Forever.

Tears splashed on her cheeks as she nodded her consent.

In a minute she'd covered Sam and sat back watching Ghaleb doing a meticulous suture, her eyes flitting from his hands to Sam's face, panic hovering at the periphery of her reactions, a black fog threatening to encroach at any moment.

She knew he was stable, couldn't be suffering from anything serious. But she still charted unforeseen complications, injuries that would reveal themselves later. When it was too late…

"There are no hidden injuries, Viv." He'd read her mind! "We're two experienced doctors with thousands of cases under our belts. We're just panicking because it's Sam. But we've dealt with his condition and have a solid clinical diagnosis. Don't let nightmares prey on your mind."

She turned her lips into his palm, let her tears fall faster, wetting it. "What would I have done without you?"

He dragged her to him over Sam's body as if to form a barrier with their bodies and love between him and harm, rested his forehead on hers. "We don't need to ever consider that question, *ya rohi.* You'll never be without me."

"He'll be fine, Viv." Ghaleb pulled Viv into his arms as they stood by the now-sleeping Sam's bedside in Intensive Care.

Sam had regained consciousness on the way to the center but had remained disoriented, couldn't remember his fall, kept asking the same questions and saying the same things over and over, post-traumatic amnesia, the inability to form and retain new memories validating their diagnosis. Once at the center a battery of tests had proved it. He was suffering from severe concussion and moderate brain edema. He would be fine in days.

Viv didn't answer, leaned into him, let him hold her, protect her, her eyes still tinged with the terror that had crushed his heart when he'd imagined Sam lying injured, his life seeping away, when he'd seen him draped over those rocks like a damaged toy.

"We'll both spend the night right here, Viv. I'll get Anna a room next door. Get into bed with Sam while I arrange it."

She nodded, her eyes brimming. He groaned, took her lips, crushed her to him, gave her what she needed—solace, strength. He'd give her, and Sam, everything he had, everything he was.

With a last lip-clinging kiss, he withdrew, swept her into his arms, carried her to Sam's side, tucked her in, bent to kiss both mother and son. His whole world.

He strode out, dread still echoing, relief descending in degrees.

An epiphany had been building to a crescendo inside him, had started changing his life since the moment he'd laid eyes on Viv again. He'd thought it had reached its climax that night at his desert hideaway.

Since then it had all been coming together like a dream. Besides the nights of transfiguring passion with Viv, everything else between them soared. She was perfection itself, not only to him as a man but to him as a prince, beyond his dreams. She provided him with insight, counsel, confidence, peace. And though she never expressed her emotions, neither did she again mention the limitation she'd imposed on the nature or time of their relationship. He felt he provided her with all the vital things she provided him, that he was invading her heart again. Adding to his growing joy was Sam, everything he'd ever dreamed of in a son. Just being hers would have made him that. Her flesh would be his, *was* his. Yet he loved Sam for himself.

Then, over the last hours, his epiphany had reached its true climax. He'd long known he'd give his life for Viv. Then he'd seen Sam hurt, had feared losing him and he'd known. He didn't only love him for being Viv's, for being himself. He far more than loved him. He'd give his life for him, too.

A month ago now, he'd fought to get Viv back in his life. Today he'd fought for Sam. He'd been ready to give anything in both fights, but he hadn't needed to. He hadn't even won those fights but had each time been handed the vital victory.

It made him feel he didn't deserve the privilege, the bliss of having it, of having Viv, and Sam.

Resolve tugged at lips as his strides widened. He hadn't deserved them.

But he would.

Viv stared at the newspaper in her trembling hand. She read the headlines and text again and again until her legs buckled.

*The Crown Prince's marriage of state. The bride to satisfy all sides decided upon and negotiations begun. The ceremony would be followed by peace treaties vital to the region.*

She couldn't deceive herself anymore.

She was going to lose him again. This time forever.

But this time she did accept it. He'd said it himself. His duties were way bigger than her or anything he felt for her.

*But he does feel for me,* her mind cried in desperation.

In the past he'd never been this magnanimous, this devoted, this vocal. He'd never made statements that tasted of forever.

*You'll never be without me.*

It must have been the poignancy of the situation, reason insisted, an unguarded exaggeration in the wake of a catastrophe averted. He couldn't have meant it the way she needed him to mean it. But, oh, God, she had to be fair. He wasn't in a position to mean it. He wasn't free to choose, even if his choice was her.

And for a while he *had* chosen her. This must be what publicizing their relationship meant. Now it would come to an end.

The two months she'd initially set were over today. She knew Ghaleb no longer believed she'd leave, not now, not ever. But she could never share him even if she could stay after he married.

*And she couldn't.* She had to leave. Now. His marriage was weeks away, and she'd already heard whispers that her presence was causing trouble, might even cause things to fall through. She couldn't have him at the price of peace, his and a whole region's. She had to leave before she made it any worse.

As for her, she'd been fooling herself. She'd never get enough of him or living with him and Sam as a family. Whether she left today or a month from now, it would all end the same way. She'd go on being a mother, a niece and a doctor, but her life as a woman would be over. She had to end it now or she'd lose her mind, living each moment dreading the end. She had to preserve her sanity and stamina—for Sam, and Anna.

Feeling her life being extinguished already, she fumbled for her phone, pushed the dial button.

In a moment a deep voice answered her. *"Sayedati?"*

"Abdur-Ruhman..." She bit her lips to stifle her sobs, rasped on. "I am in the greatest need of your help. And, please, *please*...keep it a secret from Prince Ghaleb. Until I'm gone."

Viv stood staring at the house at the end of the driveway as the cab drove away.

It was her house. It felt as if she'd never seen it before.

It felt as if her whole life before the two months in Omraania with Ghaleb had been erased.

Now she had to rebuild some new kind of life, form new memories. She *did* have much to live for. Sam. Anna. The indescribable memories Ghaleb had given her.

"Mo-*om!*"

She smiled at Sam's urgency, thanking God every moment for sparing her baby, restoring him to her. Sam had bounced back from his injury in a couple of days, had been back to normal within a week. Ghaleb had still checked him over and over before he'd given him a clean bill of health, before he'd let them all move out of the hospital and back to the palace. He'd almost never left Sam's side or hers in all that time, turning what could have been an ordeal without him into a well of incredible memories, basking in the invincibility of his affection and protection.

Sam had reveled in having Ghaleb as obsessive as her about his recovery. He couldn't get enough of Ghaleb or his attention. He'd bounded to tests as if to the most exciting outing. The last test had been two days ago…

"Mo-*om*…look, *look.*"

The excitement in Sam's voice triggered something inside her. Trepidation?

But that was silly. What could there be…?

Suddenly the vagueness crystallized into a… presence. Unmistakable. All-encompassing.

*And it couldn't possibly be here.*

She swung around. And there he was, striding away from a gleaming black limo, his wide steps consuming the width of the street between them.

*Ghaleb.*

In seconds he was looming over her, his face that of a stranger. An enraged stranger.

Then his snarl hit her, almost knocked her off her feet with its harshness. "Were you ever going to tell me?"

# CHAPTER TWELVE

VIV STARED UP AT Ghaleb in the cold twilight, her starving eyes taking in everything about him, the stark beauty of his noble face, the massive shoulders covered in a light-colored coat that deepened his dark complexion, everything inside her surging in jubilation. *He was here.*

Confusion interrupted the happiness that gushed at the gift of seeing him again. Why was he here?

Then a resurgence of the trepidation that had chilled her marrow moments ago swamped everything. He looked incensed.

Because she'd left the moment his back had been turned?

No—there was something else, something more…

*Were you ever going to tell me?*

His question slammed into her, registering at last.

Oh, God. He'd found out?

How had he found out?

*He* couldn't *find out. She had to be the one to tell him... Please...*

"Ghaleb."

She heard Sam's squeal a second before he collided into Ghaleb's legs, hugging him around his hips with all his might.

Ghaleb relieved her of his rage, his expression changing as if by magic as he bent to pick Sam up, giving him hugs and kisses of equal enthusiasm and delight.

Sam's usual inquisitiveness burst forth. "Are you staying? Will you have a vacation with us, like we had one with you? Our house isn't like yours but it's okay and we'll be together."

Ghaleb kissed him again, his face full of tenderness. "We *will* be together, Sam. I'm here to take you all back." His gaze slid to Viv, his smile slipping as rage slithered back.

Sam let out a piercing scream of joy and nearly rammed Ghaleb in the nose in another frantic hug.

Ghaleb let out a guffaw that clawed at Viv's heart as he put Sam back on the ground and went down on his haunches in front of him, his special smile for Sam nearly blinding her. "Once we're back home, Sam, we'll have lots to talk about, man to man. Now, I want you to go with Anna, get any stuff you want with you. I need to talk to your mother."

Sam gave a vigorous nod, his smile wide, then gave Ghaleb another hug. He pulled back with a hesitant look on his face, looking up at Viv in belated worry that he should have asked her consent first. Viv only stared back at him. It seemed he took her blankness as approval as he giggled and hurtled away to Anna, who was standing a few feet away, watching the reunion scene with a choked-up expression on her face.

Viv's numb gaze went from her to Ghaleb as he uncoiled to his daunting height, the affectionate light lingering in his eyes from looking at Sam and Anna draining away.

His face settled into a grim mask as he gestured for her to lead the way into her house. She did, controlled by his will, held up by his power, his vibes flaying her back, sending her emotions careening. It was only numbness that stopped her from turning around, throwing herself at him and smothering him in kisses.

The kisses that were certainly the last thing he wanted from her now. She must be losing it if longing was overpowering her dread of the impending confrontation.

Once he had her in the seclusion of her study, he burned fingerprints into her flesh as he turned her to face him.

"How——?"

He interrupted her hoarse question. "How did I get here before you? By taking advantage of one of the royal privileges you despise so much, traveling on my own jet."

She bit her lip. "I——I didn't——"

"What didn't you do, Viv?" His anger slashed across her attempt again. "You didn't make Abdur-Ruhman risk my wrath by helping you leave Omraania the moment my back was turned? You didn't use his loyalty to you, the woman who'd shown him respect and kindness, whom he felt he'd repaid by failing to ensure her son's safety, to stall me until you got away? And he did. I found out in spite of his efforts to give you a head start. What else didn't you do? You didn't leave me, on the very day you'd specified, when you knew I believed you wouldn't go, that you no longer put a time limit on our relationship, without even saying goodbye? Is this your payback for the way I once left you, Viv?"

"Please, Ghaleb…"

He grated on. "What else didn't you do, Viv? You didn't keep me in the dark?"

He *did* know. But how?

It didn't matter *how* he'd found out. He had.

"I was going to tell you—" she started.

"When, Viv?" He cut her off, pain raking across his face. "After seven more years?"

"I—I just wanted to be out of Omraania when I did…"

He took an explosive step toward her, clamped her shoulders in convulsing hands. "I asked you—and you lied to me. *Ya Ullah*—you *lied*. But you couldn't lie to my heart. It felt the connection, the bond, the blood running in his veins calling to mine from the first moment. But Sam's resemblance to you, and your silence, then your lies, threw me. Still, the more I knew and loved him, the more I saw myself in him. The expressions, the physique, the temperament, the tastes and talents. Then he was in danger and I knew I would die for him, even when I still thought he was only yours, by another man. But during our stay in the center, the truth kept beating down on me. I thought it was a crazy doubt, a crazier hope, that you couldn't possibly hide the truth of my son from me, but it got so maddening that I had to find out, once and for all. That last test I performed on Sam was a DNA test. *I had to find out through a DNA test that I have a son, Viv.*"

Tears spilled then, scouring her cheeks, scorching her lips.

"I found from his official papers that his name is Sammy. Is it some sort of nickname for Samuel or is it the Arabic name?"

She nodded, sending her tears splashing over her hands and his. Sammy meant elevated, superior in Arabic. "I—I wanted him to have a name from your heritage but one that wouldn't sound too foreign here."

He closed his eyes on a spasm of emotion.

Hard-breathing moments passed before his snarl slashed her again. "How could you let me keep thinking Sam wasn't mine? How could you deprive me of my son? And Sam of his father?"

That stopped the flow of tears—the sheer injustice of the accusation. She straightened, resurrected anger and misery storming through her. "Because I couldn't raise Sam's hopes when that father could never acknowledge him."

He seemed to grow bigger, scowling down at her, biting out his words between gritted teeth.

"You're implying it's even a possibility I'd deny my own flesh and blood?"

"How should I have known what you would have done, Ghaleb?" she hurled right back. "You treated me like a dirty secret, then just like dirt when you left me. For all I knew, you could have considered Sam a catastrophe to be kept hidden at all costs, might have never wanted to know about him and feared that other people would find out. I was protecting him. I only came to Omraania because he kept asking about his father, because I had to make a decision about whether you deserved to know about him or if I should tell him his father is dead."

Viv's words hit Ghaleb like a decapitating sword.

An explosion of remorse and shame followed, snuffing all anger and disillusion.

How could he have forgotten for a second what he'd done to her? How could he have dared blame her for anything?

But he had forgotten, had blamed her for the eighteen hours since he'd held the DNA test results in his hand. All he'd been able to think had been that he'd been denied his son, that Viv had left, leaving him without her, without Sam.

But in a few words she'd torn aside the mask of strength, the coating of invulnerability she wore so seamlessly, and had held up her wounds for him to take a good look at. The wounds he'd inflicted. *She would have told Sam his father—he—was dead.*

And he would have deserved it.

But no. He'd only deserved it before. Now, after all that had happened between them, after he'd lavished all of himself on her, how could she still think the same? Why had she left him? *She still couldn't love him again. She never would.*

He staggered back, dropped onto the first surface that broke his momentum, a couch, dropped his head in his hands.

He felt her sag onto a chair facing him.

Hope still beat at him, possessing a crazy life of its own, sprouting where it shouldn't, insisting on fighting for survival.

He raised his head, his gaze pouring aching and longing over her beloved face, finding it pinched and stricken.

"Viv…" he rasped. "Has nothing changed your mind? Not even us becoming lovers again?"

A minute passed until he thought she'd

ignored his question. Then she let out a shuddering exhalation.

"Going to Omraania, learning your situation, has only shown me how duty rules your life, that you could never acknowledge Sam publicly." She looked away. "And what did becoming temporary lovers have to do with it?"

He couldn't dodge the "temporary" stab. It sank through his heart. He let out a hoarse whisper. "I thought you'd come to know me better, that you might have changed your view of me."

Her eyes snapped back to him, wide, urgent. "I did. I am certain now you'll make Sam the most wonderful father, that he's the luckiest boy on earth to have you."

Hope surged, almost bursting his shriveling heart. "You think that?" Suddenly anger and anguish crashed back. And he roared again. "Then why didn't you tell me? Why did you leave?"

Tears surged from eyes so reddened he had a horrible mental image that they'd spill blood at any moment.

"I couldn't tell you—couldn't… I had to be away from you when I did…and I *had* to leave. You don't have a place in your public life for Sam. I couldn't compromise you. But I *was* going to tell you everything, Ghaleb, today…but you beat me to it. My plan was to resume my life here, let you handle this as it best suited you, let him know you're his father, be part of his life if you could, as I am now certain you want to be."

Every word of her explanation detonated in his mind.

She'd gone through all those ordeals not only without his support and love but suffering his estrangement and humiliation. She would have gone on shouldering the burden of being a single parent, counting on nothing from him but occasional visits and peripheral support. He was certain she wouldn't have accepted even financial help. Not for herself anyway.

It was too much. *Too much.*

He lowered his eyes, wondering if guilt and self-loathing would have eaten a visible hole through his heart by now.

But that was more selfishness and self-indulgence.

Strength flooded him, along with the determination to defend her, to worship her with every breath left in him. He rose to his feet.

He came to stand above her, made his pledge. "Sam will not only know I am his father, will not only have me in his life—he'll have me there for him every second of mine."

She shook her head. "How can that be when—?"

He cut across her confusion, made the offer of his life, offering his very life. "Marry me, Viv."

This was it. She'd lost her mind. She was having delusions.

Ghaleb couldn't be standing here, asking—asking…

Then understanding crushed her.

Ghaleb, who'd never wanted her for more than his temporary mistress, was forced to offer her marriage now to have the son she now realized how fiercely he wanted.

He was offering her a marriage of convenience.

Alongside the one he was duty bound to enter into?

Did he think she could survive being in his life, an unwanted burden, sharing him with another woman? *She couldn't.*

She groped for a way out. Some middle ground. Something where she wouldn't shrivel up and die.

"You don't have to go as far as that to have Sam, Ghaleb," she choked. "I—I heard that in your culture the children of a prince born out of wedlock are still considered part of the royal family. For Sam's sake, I'll live in Omraania so you can have constant access to him, and he to you."

He seemed to be getting larger with every word out of her mouth, until she almost whimpered. Oh, God, she'd only managed to enrage him further. He now looked every bit the ruthless sheikh, the implacable desert raider, one capable of extreme actions and pitiless punishment, exacting an eye for an eye. What if her refusal pushed him to do something drastic?

*What if he took Sam away?*

He took two strides closer to pour his wrath over her. "Isn't it enough you kept Sam from me all these years, and especially these last weeks? You now dare suggest I'd let him be some lower-rank royal from an illegitimate union? No, Viv, and this *is* a decree. He will be my rightful heir, from a legitimate union. Ours. You *will* marry me."

She shook her head, desperation suffocating her, the abyss that had long lain at her feet yawning, sucking her in.

And she screamed, *"But if I marry you, I'll die!"*

\* \* \*

Ghaleb shuddered as her scream seemed to bounce off the walls.

He watched her weeping, felt chunks of himself falling away, sanity and strength seeping out.

Then it burst out of him, the insupportable, uncontainable agony. *"You hate me that much?"*

"I *love* you that much," she screamed.

Everything stilled, vanished. Nothing remained but the echo of her words, the confession that had blasted out of her heart to pulverize his. He swayed, the joy too brutal to withstand, too huge to encompass. She loved him. She *loved* him.

*Loved him.*

And incomparable, obliviously cruel, she was going on. "But whatever you feel for me, it isn't love, and then you'll marry that other woman, as you're bound to do, and I'd go mad being near you. What kind of mother would I be for Sam then?"

He fell to his knees at her feet, where he'd long thrown everything that he was, honor and belief, hopes and future, heart and soul, all his power.

Would he ever realize the scope of his crimes against her? Would he ever convince her of the totality of her ownership of him? After he'd left her living in the agony of such misconception, the hell of such doubt and desperation?

*How had her love for him remained intact through it all?*

He lowered his forehead to her knees, as if in deepest prayer. He *was* praying, in searing humbleness and gratitude, for the immeasurable gift of her love.

Her quaking hands tried to push his head away. He clung to her, to dear life. "Viv, *ya aghla'n'naas*—and you are, the most precious one in the world. You *are* my world…"

*"I'll marry you."*

The desperation in her cry was like a slap. He did welcome any abuse she'd serve out to him, but if she kept doing this to him, he might not live long enough to pay penance. "Viv…"

She squeezed his hand, staying his groan. "On one condition. That as soon as you legitimize Sam, you divorce me."

He had to stop her before she killed him. She and Sam must have him, alive for decades to come.

He rose, enveloping the hands she tried to wrench out of his hold. "I have a better plan, *ya hayati*—and you *are* my life. I *will* marry you.

And I'll never divorce you. I can't, not for Sam's sake but for mine. I would die without you."

Her face crumpled with such suffering that he lost it, snatched her up in his arms, crushed her to him, stormed kisses all over her, stilling her quaking lips in his in his desperation to convince her. "*Ahebbek, ya,* Viv, I love you, *ya roh galbi…*"

She sagged in his arms, let him kiss her, her tears now a heavy stream. "Please, Ghaleb. You don't have to say you love me…"

He took his arms off her, took three strides away, seething with frustration, then swung back to her and shouted, "*Ana aabodek*—I *worship* you."

He brought himself under instant control, approached her again, let love tremble on a coaxing smile. "You want proof? I'll give you proof every day of our lives. But as a first and hopefully conclusive proof, I will not enter a marriage of state, not now, not ever. I will marry you, be yours alone forever, and I will never, ever let you go. Even death will not break my vows."

Viv pulled back, her tears ebbing, her mouth dropping open. The look Ghaleb gave her shook the foundations of her soul.

"How?" she whispered.

"Easily. On my part, that is. The duty that ruled my life, that won over my love for you seven years ago, lost out this time. No contest. I destroyed seven years of your life for Omraania. Missed the first six precious years of Sam's life doing my duty. And I'm done. I'm not sacrificing seven more seconds of your or Sam's life, for any reason. It is the crown prince's duty to marry for his kingdom and I'm no longer that prince. That was the hard part. Convincing my father and the tribune of elders to bypass me for my younger brother, Essam."

"Oh, God…"

"I hope you won't be too disappointed you won't be the future queen of Omraania. Not that there has ever been much hope of that. I truly believe my father will outlive us all. It probably would have been Sam who would have become king. Now my brother's son will be."

She gasped like a fish out of water. "But—but you…*you can't!*"

"I can, I did, and I couldn't be happier."

She suddenly took hold of his face in frantic hands. "You can't give up your birthright. I'm sorry, sorry, sorry. I believe that you love me, I'll be your second wife, or anything at all. You have to take it back!"

He turned his mouth into her clutching hands. "What I want to take back, what I'd give my life to be able to erase, is the hurt I caused you, the seven years I caused us to lose. I will never let anything come between us again for a second."

"How can you say that? You're a prince, you have a duty…"

"I have a destiny, and that's you," he asserted with all the gravity of another unbreakable vow. "And I was born a prince, but I *chose* to be a doctor. But medicine is more than my vocation. It's what brought us together, what will ensure we'll stay together all the time, doing what we do best, doing the most good as only we could."

"Ghaleb, please, don't," she choked out, her tears again a constant stream with the enormity of it all. "You don't need to prove anything more to me. I believe you and in you. As for Sam—"

A fierce kiss stopped her. "I would do this if we didn't have Sam, if you'd been unable to have children at all. Believe *this*. Sam, as irreplaceable as he is, isn't the reason I did this. It's all for you. Want more proof that I want you, only you, would die for you, will live for you? I will leave the *essmuh* in your hands in our marriage."

The blows were coming in too fast. She swayed in his arms, gasped her incomprehension, "The *essmuh*...?"

"In my faith, that means you'll have total control of the marriage, our children and even my assets. It's you who'll decide to keep me or if you ever don't want to, you'll have the power to divorce me."

She sagged onto his chest, heaving sobs of incredulity, of elation, of shock. "Ghaleb...too much..."

He hugged her fiercely, vowed again, "Nothing will ever be too much, *ya roh galbi,* not for you."

"I—I... Oh, my love, Ghaleb, oh, God...are you sure?"

"My love for you is the only certainty in my life."

Suddenly her tremors stopped and resolve flooded through her. She pushed out of his hold, took him by the arms. "Then you'll understand that I'm certain, too, Ghaleb. I want you to take it back. My only agony was thinking you didn't love me. But now I know you do, it changes everything. You'd die for me and you think I wouldn't for you? I *would* give my life for you.

Giving up anything else so you'd do your duty is so much less, something I'll accept, live with, now I know your heart is mine."

His lips twisted as he gave her a look of mock hurt. "So you can give up having me exclusively? You don't think that's a big thing, do you? You don't mind sharing me?"

A stab of jealousy impaled her. She bit her lip on the agony.

"Oh, God, don't," she quavered. "You know what I mean."

"Don't be so sure. I've never suffered insecurity except on your account. And it's almost destroyed me. I need every proof, with every breath, of how much I mean to you. In fact, I just handed you the upper hand, left myself totally powerless and in desperate need of reassurance."

She attacked him with an almost violent kiss. "How about seven years' worth of loving you, of being alive only for our son? I would have continued to exist only because I had him, part of you with me. How's that for reassurance? How's that for proof of your total power over me?"

"I don't know." His eyes sparkled at her with the joy of unshed tears. "You see, by giving you the *essmuh* I have given everything to you. I now have to await your mercy in asking for *my* hand in marriage."

Humbled by the enormity of what he'd given up, what he was offering, delirious at her belief in his boundless love, she squirmed out of his embrace, knelt before him, snatching his hands in hers, burying kisses and tears and love in them. "I beg for you, my love. For anything and everything you want to give. I am yours, have always been, will always be. Throughout this life and, if I have anything to say about it, beyond."

He joined her on the floor, curving his whole body around her, mashing his face into hers, mingling his tears with hers.

She finally lay huddled with him in the aftermath of almost losing each other again. She trembled with the reprieve, with the expectation of a life of joy, trepidation at feeling so much, having so much still quaking through her. She felt Ghaleb tense up. Her heart punched against her ribs.

"What is it?"

"I didn't know a man was allowed to have that much happiness. Then you went silent and all the doubts and fears attacked me again, *ya habibati.*"

She groaned, hugged him tighter. "You do feel insecure about me, don't you? An hour ago I thought it an impossibility, thought the depth of my involvement was transparent." She took her arms away, reached up to brace her hands on his massive shoulders. "Give it up, now, all doubts and worry and silliness that I can be anything but yours, happily, deliriously, every second and forever. I am invoking my power over you." She arched one eyebrow at him, teasing. "May I remind you I have the *essmuh* in my hands."

Ghaleb gave her her ultimate reward, the sight of his unfettered happiness, the sound of his overjoyed laughter.

He swept her into his arms and she struggled to hold back a new flood of tears. There'd been enough tears. Not even tears of bliss were allowed now. She looked up at him, opening herself wide open for him to see everything she felt for him, felt his adoration radiating from him for her to soar into its limitless horizon.

"About this *essmuh* stuff..." She nipped his jaw playfully, drew his instant groan of pleasure. "In control, huh? Sounds kinky." She trailed a fingernail from his face to his chest to his abdomen and...lower, then purred, "I can work with that."

He let out a laugh that sent fireworks and rainbows bursting throughout her universe. "I always knew you had a vivid imagination."

Just then Sam burst in. Anna stood at the door, shrugging her helplessness to stop him.

Ghaleb motioned for them to come in. "I hope it's all right with you to have me permanently in your life, Anna. As a son-in-law. Viv has just asked for my hand in marriage."

He quirked one eyebrow at Viv. She only took said hand to her lips and smothered it in kisses.

Anna put both hands to her lips, her face contorting with emotion, her eyes gushing with tears of happiness. "Oh, Ghaleb, Vivienne. Oh, my darlings, this is the happiest day of my life."

Sam, who didn't understand the import of asking hands in marriage and sons-in-law, jumped up and down, coming to his own conclusions. "You're laughing and kissing. You made up. Yes?"

Ghaleb opened his arms to him. "Oh, yes. And how."

In a second Sam was all arms and legs over both of them. Laughing, Viv swept him into her embrace, then Ghaleb swept both of them in his.

Giving her a kiss that again pledged all he was to her, he turned to Sam, who was watching them with enraptured eyes.

"Now, Sam, we have a very long story to tell you. One that has the happiest ending. And it's just beginning, too…"

₽ς

# MEDICAL™

## Large Print

### *Titles for the next six months…*

## June

| | |
|---|---|
| A MUMMY FOR CHRISTMAS | Caroline Anderson |
| A BRIDE AND CHILD WORTH WAITING FOR | Marion Lennox |
| ONE MAGICAL CHRISTMAS | Carol Marinelli |
| THE GP'S MEANT-TO-BE BRIDE | Jennifer Taylor |
| THE ITALIAN SURGEON'S CHRISTMAS MIRACLE | Alison Roberts |
| CHILDREN'S DOCTOR, CHRISTMAS BRIDE | Lucy Clark |

## July

| | |
|---|---|
| THE GREEK DOCTOR'S NEW-YEAR BABY | Kate Hardy |
| THE HEART SURGEON'S SECRET CHILD | Meredith Webber |
| THE MIDWIFE'S LITTLE MIRACLE | Fiona McArthur |
| THE SINGLE DAD'S NEW-YEAR BRIDE | Amy Andrews |
| THE WIFE HE'S BEEN WAITING FOR | Dianne Drake |
| POSH DOC CLAIMS HIS BRIDE | Anne Fraser |

## August

| | |
|---|---|
| CHILDREN'S DOCTOR, SOCIETY BRIDE | Joanna Neil |
| THE HEART SURGEON'S BABY SURPRISE | Meredith Webber |
| A WIFE FOR THE BABY DOCTOR | Josie Metcalfe |
| THE ROYAL DOCTOR'S BRIDE | Jessica Matthews |
| OUTBACK DOCTOR, ENGLISH BRIDE | Leah Martyn |
| SURGEON BOSS, SURPRISE DAD | Janice Lynn |

MILLS & BOON®
*Pure reading pleasure*™

0509 LP 2P P1 Medical

# MEDICAL™

## ─⎍─ *Large Print* ─⎍─

### September

| | |
|---|---|
| THE CHILDREN'S DOCTOR'S SPECIAL PROPOSAL | Kate Hardy |
| ENGLISH DOCTOR, ITALIAN BRIDE | Carol Marinelli |
| THE DOCTOR'S BABY BOMBSHELL | Jennifer Taylor |
| EMERGENCY: SINGLE DAD, MOTHER NEEDED | Laura Iding |
| THE DOCTOR CLAIMS HIS BRIDE | Fiona Lowe |
| ASSIGNMENT: BABY | Lynne Marshall |

### October

| | |
|---|---|
| A FAMILY FOR HIS TINY TWINS | Josie Metcalfe |
| ONE NIGHT WITH HER BOSS | Alison Roberts |
| TOP-NOTCH DOC, OUTBACK BRIDE | Melanie Milburne |
| A BABY FOR THE VILLAGE DOCTOR | Abigail Gordon |
| THE MIDWIFE AND THE SINGLE DAD | Gill Sanderson |
| THE PLAYBOY FIREFIGHTER'S PROPOSAL | Emily Forbes |

### November

| | |
|---|---|
| THE SURGEON SHE'S BEEN WAITING FOR | Joanna Neil |
| THE BABY DOCTOR'S BRIDE | Jessica Matthews |
| THE MIDWIFE'S NEW-FOUND FAMILY | Fiona McArthur |
| THE EMERGENCY DOCTOR CLAIMS HIS WIFE | Margaret McDonagh |
| THE SURGEON'S SPECIAL DELIVERY | Fiona Lowe |
| A MOTHER FOR HIS TWINS | Lucy Clark |

MILLS & BOON®
*Pure reading pleasure*™

0509 LP 2P P2 Medical